Solve by Christmas

By Amber Schamel

I0586658

Dedication

To my 11 siblings who have been so patient, supportive,
understanding...and unknowingly inspiration for the characters
and humor in my books.

And to my parents who help me solve all of life's mysteries.

©2017 by Amber Schamel
Library of Congress#
http://www.AmberSchamel.com
Published by Vision Writer Publications
200 S. Wilcox St. #328
Castle Rock, CO 80104

Paperback edition created 2017
ISBN 978-0-9991767-2-6

All Scriptures quotations are taken from the King James Version (Public Domain).
Quotations from historical folksong *Workers of the World Awaken* written by Joe Hill 1910 (Public Domain).
Cover images from Shutterstock.com
Cover Design by Roseanna White Designs
Other photos from 123RF Stock Photo and Public Domain.

By Amber Schamel

Table of Contents

By Amber Schamel

Acknowledgments

First of all, I would like to thank my Lord and Savior, Jesus Christ. He is the real Author; I am merely a vessel. I have seen His hand at work every step of the way. In truth, the only thing that's good in me is Jesus.

I would also like to thank my family, my critique partners, my cover designer, Roseanna White, and so many others have helped make this story into what it is. I am so thankful for each of these individuals! If I tried to mention them all and thank them as they deserve, it would take a book of its own. I cannot thank them enough for the investment that they've made into my life and writing.

A special thank you to my editor, Deirdre Lockhart, whose encouragement and advice have helped make this book everything it could be.

But most of all, a HUGE THANK YOU to all of my friends and readers! This project would be impossible without your support! Thank you for caring, reading, sharing, and your encouraging words. The fact that you would take time out of your day to read my work or send me a comment is such an honor for me. By sharing these stories with your friends, you have given me the greatest compliment possible.

THANK YOU!

By Amber Schamel

Author's Note

Thank you for joining me in my first-ever mystery! I hope you enjoy it.

Solve by Christmas deals with a very sensitive issue, that of depression and suicide. This has become a worldwide epidemic and one of the leading causes of death in all ages, but especially the ages of 10-24. My prayer is that through Jasper and Mr. Rudin's story, you will come to know the hope and joy that is to be found in Jesus Christ and the power of His Holy Spirit. For it is as the street preacher said, "When your life is no longer worth living, when you're washed up with nothing left, give your life to Christ, and He will give you His. What an exchange that is, my friend! Because He lives, our lives have meaning. Perhaps you've believed there is no reason. There is no hope. But Christ died to give you a different path. Not our works. Not what others say we are. Not what we say we are. But what the King of

5

Heaven and Earth says we are. You may say you're a failure. Others may agree. But Christ says you're worth everything, and His is the judgment that counts."

If you have not yet discovered this hope, I would be glad to introduce you to the power that changed my life and made it worth living.

Or if you would merely like someone to bind with you in prayer, whether it is for yourself or someone you love, my family and I would be honored to pray with and for you. I can also add you to our church prayer list if you so desire.

Feel free to contact me through my website, http://www.amberschamel.com/, or send me an email to author@amberschamel.com.

Also, if you have been contemplating suicide, I hope you will take the time to watch this youtube video today. https://youtu.be/XAVRdPYG9NQ

Your life has meaning. You are worth more than 10,000 worlds like this one. Please, do not take your life.

Chapter One

Denver, December 1, 1913

At last, Jasper Hollock, Private Investigator, was going to get his first real case. He cleared his throat to keep from letting out a whoop as he jumped from the trolley and dodged traffic across Broadway. After two years of monotonous union cases, it was about time. One of these days, he'd put criminals behind bars instead of employees out of work. This day would be his first step toward the destiny God had ordained for him.

His overcoat streamed behind him as his long strides carried him toward the Rudin Sugar Company building. The brick structure loomed ahead, lined with windows across the middle and top floors. A flash of movement signaled the employees were about to begin the day's work.

Shoving his left hand into his pocket, he ensured the note was still present before opening the glass double door and slipping out of the cold. He'd come as soon as Denny appeared at his apartment door with the note. Dare say, he probably beat the errand boy back to the factory—hardly a fair brag considering he paid the trolley fee while the poor adolescent rode his bicycle through the slushy streets. But he needed to get more facts. The janitor's short explanation was not anywhere near enough.

Details, people. Details. Didn't they know life and death could be found in details?

He mounted the stairs two at a time to the second floor. Mr. Rudin's secretary glanced up from his papers as Jasper passed. "Morning, Mr. Hollock."

"Detective Hollock, if you don't mind. Would you be so kind as to let Mr. Rudin know I must speak with him directly? I'm to take a look upstairs, and afterward, I will need to speak with him."

The man raised an eyebrow above his monocle. "Already done, *detective*. I was just about to send for you."

Jasper halted and turned around. "Were you?"

"Indeed. It appears Mr. Rudin would like to speak with you as well. Shall I show you in?" The elder man placed both his palms on the desk as if to rise.

"No, I have a short order of business first." Spinning on his heel, Jasper continued down the hall. He could feel the secretary's glare on his back. Old Mr. Stosch liked to keep things prompt, but this couldn't wait.

Turning down another corridor, Jasper came upon the janitor standing sentry over the factory laboratory door, mop in hand. The man's shoulders loosened, and his mop wavered. "There you are, Detective Hollock."

"Now, now, Charlie. What's all this? You said next to nothing in your note."

"I couldn't, sir. Didn't want to raise an alarm without talking to you first." The mop of hair on his head rivaled the one in his hand. He brushed gray strands out of his eyes. "I was coming to mop up before the boys begin, and I found the door ajar."

Jasper chewed the inside of his cheek. The laboratory doors were never left unlocked, much less open. "Any sign of tampering?"

"None. Well..." Charlie's eyes flitted to the doorway. "Leastwise as far as I can tell."

Crouching to examine the knob and lock, Jasper searched the metal surface for scratches. After pulling his magnifier from his pocket, he held it up to the lock and surrounding area. He puffed a hot breath against it, but no grease or finger marks appeared. Curious, indeed.

"Detective, I locked up on Friday night, I know I did. I just can't understand how it would have been open."

Jasper took his time before standing. He patted Charlie's shoulder. "Not to worry, man. We'll get it sorted out."

A sugary scent wafted through the room. Bright lights dangling from the ceiling gleamed on countless shelved glass vials, and various pieces of equipment standing at attention on desks lined up in smart rows—a drawer on one end hung partially ajar.

"Are you the only one with a key, Charlie?"

"The lab manager has one. And Mr. Rudin, of course."

The windows along the far wall, facing Broadway, appeared neither broken nor tampered with, but a round splotch of wet darkened the wooden boards. The wetness stretched from the original site to the window and back again to the door. Charlie had apparently mopped up. "Was there some kind of spill in here recently?"

"Not that they've mentioned. I'm thinking it was done when whoever it was snooped around. There was a broken vial, too."

Interesting. Jasper tucked that piece of information away for later. He took a brief stroll around the room. "Is this window usually left unlocked?"

Charlie's boots squeaked as he crossed the floor. "No, I don't see why it should be. Do you think the perpetrator came in that way? Then snuck out the door? That'd explain why it was open after I left it locked."

Lifting the window frame, Jasper peered out. "How would one get up here without being seen from the street? Is there roof access somehow?"

"Dunno. I haven't paid much attention. I guess I could go up and take a look."

"Details, Charlie. Details. They're important." Jasper pulled his head back inside and shut the window securely. "When will the lab manager be in?"

"He usually comes in around nine, I believe."

Jasper flipped open his pocket watch. Eight thirty-five. "I will have to return to question him then. Lock it up, won't you? No one besides the manager comes in until I return. Understood?"

By Amber Schamel

"Yes, sir." Charlie's chest puffed out. "No one in but him."

"Thatta boy." Jasper gave the janitor a nod and headed toward Mr. Rudin's office. He could always think better when walking. If someone had broken into the lab, what might they want? And what harm could come to Mr. Rudin's company because of it? Whatever the intent, Jasper would stop it before any harm touched his dear old patron.

"Could Mr. Rudin beg an audience with you now, Detective Hollock?"

Jasper rolled his eyes at the secretary's sarcastic tone. "I'll forgive you, Mr. Stosch. I couldn't expect a secretary to understand matters of more pressing consequence than newspaper advertisements."

Mr. Stosch folded the newspaper he'd been perusing and straightened his monocle. The man's drooping brown eyes reminded him of an old hound. Perhaps it was a result of reading too many newspapers. "I read the newspaper by Mr. Rudin's request, Mr. Hollock." He stood and opened the door to the proprietor's office. "Mr. Rudin, Detective Hollock to see you."

"Yes, well, show him in. Oh, but come here a moment, Stosch." Mr. Rudin waved them inside as he crossed from a filing cabinet. Half a grin hid under his curled white mustache, and instead of sitting, he rocked back and forth on his heels. "Do close the door."

Jasper claimed the chair facing the desk and crossed one leg over his knee. Mr. Rudin was robust as ever, except for the lines between his eyebrows. Perhaps he hadn't slept well.

Mr. Rudin gripped the back of the leather chair he stood

11

behind. "Stosch, I was thinking."

The secretary clasped his hands behind his back. "Yes, sir."

"It is December the first today, getting right on toward Christmas. I'd like to give a little something to each of the employees. A gift of sorts. What do you recommend?" He leaned forward and extracted a candy from the dish on the corner of his desk.

"Well, sir, most workers would be pleased to get an early leave for the holiday."

Mr. Rudin popped the candy in his mouth. "Quite right, but I expected to give them something tangible. Some memento of my appreciation for them. Perhaps a golden coin or something."

Jasper smiled as he studied the elder man. Mr. Rudin was just that type of fellow. He'd been considerate and kind to Jasper's mother when she arrived in Denver with nothing more than the clothes on her back and the babe in her arms. What would they have done if the Rudins hadn't taken her in as housekeeper? Since then, the sugar baron had been like a father, teaching him how to golf and even shoot. With a pistol very much like the one now sitting in the man's leather chair. How odd.

"Thank you, Stosch. That is all for now." After the door closed behind the secretary, Mr. Rudin's gaze shifted to Jasper. He pressed his lips together. "My boy, I have a new case for you."

A grin spread across Jasper's face. This was it. The moment he'd been waiting for. His employer would reveal some secret stolen from the lab, and he'd have his first case of any consequence.

Rudin took a breath and stepped around his chair. "I will warn you ahead of time…it won't be an easy one."

"I can handle it, sir."

One white brow rose above Mr. Rudin's deep-set eyes. "I'm a hard case."

Jasper frowned. "Sir?"

Bending down, Mr. Rudin picked up the revolver. "I've struck a deal with God, Jasper, and you're my angel."

By Amber Schamel

Chapter Two

Jasper studied the man's face. He'd never seen Mr. Rudin so solemn. He gave his head a shake. "I'm sorry, sir, I don't follow."

The old man turned the revolver over in his hand and then sank into the leather chair. "Do you know what my life has come to, Jasper? A dead end. I have everything I dreamed of as a young man, and now that I'm old, I have never been more unhappy." He looked up, his eyes misting over. "I have a business, money, family, and yet in all of that, I find no success. No peace. You can't imagine what that is like. I have nothing left to live for."

After a long moment, he returned to his study of the weapon. "I was going to use this last night. Mr. Stosch would have found a messy sight this morning. But I thought for too long, and my Orthodox side got the best of me. Do you think God allows for suicide, Jasper boy?"

"Suicide? Mr. Rudin—"

The man held up a wrinkled hand. "I have come to a resolution." His hand went for the candy dish again. He plucked a red and white peppermint. "These are very good, you know. Made by the confectionery down the street with Rudin sugar." He stared at the piece in silence.

"Sir, I—"

"Ah yes, I was saying, I have come to a resolution. If God does not approve of my method, then I will give Him a chance to change my mind. Jasper, I am giving you until Christmas to gather evidence and convince me my life is still worth living. Of course, I'm a tough one to bargain with at times, so I do not want you to feel any personal responsibility for the outcome of this case."

"You…" Jasper tugged his left ear and took a deep breath. "You want me to…convince you to live? In twenty-four days?"

Mr. Rudin's mustache twitched. "Very good summary. You get an 'A'. I always knew you were a smart boy."

Head spinning, Jasper flopped against the backrest. How had Mr. Rudin become depressed enough to contemplate this? And lands sakes, how was he supposed to stop him?

"Now, was there something else you wanted to speak with me about?" His usual half-smile returned.

Jasper's mind had never been so muddled. "Uh, no, not at this time, sir."

"Very well, then. We both have work to do." Mr. Rudin grasped a pen and sifted through the stack on his desk.

Generally, Jasper considered himself an intelligent person.

By Amber Schamel

But at the moment, he couldn't claim that at all. Dumbfounded, he stood and shuffled out of the office.

Stosch raised one brow over the newspaper he'd returned to. "Are you ill?"

"I might be." All he wanted was to sit and gather his wits. If a boy had tripped on his way out of a candy store, his goods could not be more scattered than Jasper's thoughts. But he couldn't relax in front of Stosch. Something about the man simply irked him. "Send for me if Mr. Rudin does anything…uh…strange."

Stosch rolled his eyes and whipped the paper back up.

Escaping around the corner, Jasper loosened his tie. He quickened his pace, his mind clearing with each step. He found the washroom and shut himself inside. Bracing his hands against the wall, he took three deep breaths.

There, much better.

He turned the faucet handle and splashed cool water on his face. He stared at the water dripping from his sharp nose in the mirror's reflection. "So, Detective Hollock, greedy for your first case and look what you've got."

If he wanted high stakes, this was it. If Mr. Rudin followed through on his plan, Jasper would be *alone*. He gripped the sink to steady himself. How could so much fear be attached to one word?

The last time these sensations coursed through his veins was the thundery night his mother died. Five years ago, and he'd become more of a recluse than ever. Of course, his oddities would prevent him from gaining friends even if he tried. Mr.

By Amber Schamel

Rudin was the only other person in the world who understood him and accepted him for who he was. He couldn't let this happen. He'd protect Mr. Rudin with his own life if necessary.

What a turn of events. He'd expected Mr. Rudin to talk to him about the laboratory break-in.

The laboratory. What about that? He hadn't determined the motive behind that, either. Mr. Rudin may be in more danger than he realized.

Jasper refilled his depleted lungs. He'd interview the lab manager first. Then he'd figure out a plan to dissuade Mr. Rudin and get to the bottom of this intrusion.

He jerked open the washroom door to see Denny, the errand boy, standing there with his fist poised to knock. A smile that could win a million dollars split the young man's face. "Oh, hello, detective. Nice to see you."

What kind of kid greets you that way coming out of the washroom? Strange. This boy was strange.

"Greetings." Jasper sidestepped the boy and headed toward the lab. The boy's shoes clomped behind him.

"Did you find anything in the laboratory?"

"Vials, desks, everything you'd expect to find in such a room."

"I mean clues, Detective Hollock. Did you find any clues? I bet you sniffed out the entire scandal by now just like Sherlock Holmes does over in England."

Jasper rolled his eyes. "You do know Holmes is a fictional character. He doesn't actually live and work in the streets of London."

"Of course, I know that." Denny trotted to catch up with him. "That's why I like you. You're a real-life Sherlock. Well, at least, I think you are. You haven't actually proved it yet, since I haven't seen you work."

"Speaking of work, isn't that what you're supposed to be doing?"

Denny flashed his grin again. "Why sure, and I am. I was supposed to find you and let you know the lab manager arrived. Charlie said you'd want to talk with him."

"Brilliant. I was just headed his way." Lengthening his strides, Jasper stalked toward the lab, Denny dogging him all the way.

Charlie stood at his post as instructed. He jerked his head toward the door. "Kendal is inside."

Jasper halted in the doorframe. The lab manager clawed through a bottom file drawer, his hair tousled and his unbuttoned sleeves flapping.

"Anything missing?" Jasper asked.

"Aha! Here it is." The man dropped into a chair, his arms falling limply to his sides. "I was afraid they'd taken information, but everything seems to be accounted for."

"Nothing at all is missing?"

The man squinted around the room. "Not that I can tell. I'll continue taking inventory, but it seems all is unharmed."

After pulling a notepad from his pocket, Jasper tapped a pencil to the page. "Any idea who may have tried to get in here? What reason would someone have to invade?"

"We have documented our methods for quality control. I

suppose someone might want that, but I've no idea who."

Jasper strode to the far end of the counter and slid open a drawer. He'd seen one ajar as he entered earlier. "What is contained in here?"

"Mundane daily reports, mostly." The manager waved his hand. "Nothing anyone would want."

Reports, yes, but more than that was inside. Pencils, empty log sheets, and supplies. Nothing of much consequence on the surface, but perhaps with more clues it may play a part. He jotted down a note and closed the drawer.

"Have you had any incidents with lab workers recently?" Jasper returned his gaze to the manager.

"No, everyone seems happy." The man tucked his chin and lowered his tone. "They get paid pretty well, so no one complains."

"Any illnesses, mishaps someone might want to erase from records?"

Kendal shook his head.

"Charlie tells me you possess one of three keys to this room. Have you allowed any other workers use of it?"

"No, detective. I keep it on my person at all times. I unlock the door when I arrive and lock it when I leave. They've no call to need inside at any other time."

"I noticed a spill on the floor this morning. What substance was left overnight?" Jasper pointed to the blotch on the wooden floor.

"Sugar water with a bit of a chemical to test it. Nothing dangerous or mysterious about it. My guess is the intruder

By Amber Schamel

somehow upset it."

"I see." He notated that, too. "Very well, I will allow you to get on with your work. Please let me know if you remember anything further or discover something missing."

Pocketing his notebook, he strode out of the room. He'd done his duty at the scene. Now he'd take his quandaries before the Council of Mirrors.

Solve by Christmas

By Amber Schamel

Chapter Three

A shrill wind batted at Jasper's overcoat as he opened the black iron gate of the Montgomery Apartments. Already someone had wrapped evergreen boughs along the top. He slipped through and trotted up the steps to the main entrance. Yanking the door open, he ducked inside and then shut out the draft.

"Hello, Detective Hollock. It's about time you got here."

Jasper whirled around, his overcoat thwacking the errand boy's long legs. "Denny? What are you doing here?"

"Mr. Rudin said you were working on an important case, so I dropped by to see if you needed anything. Where have you been?"

The nerve of this boy. Choosing to ignore the insolent question, Jasper changed the subject. "Do you make a habit of stalking all of Mr. Rudin's employees?"

"No, sir, just you. Although I think I'd be good at it." A

dimple appeared in the boy's cheek, and his eyes squinted with his grin. "Company spy is almost like a company detective, right?"

Lord, give me patience. If this boy weren't an orphan, Jasper would have boxed his ears and thrown him out with a good warning to get back to his duties. With a shake of his head, he made for the stairs.

Denny followed. "Is the case difficult? Does it have to do with Charlie's note this morning? I saw you poking around the lab. Do you think someone stole something?"

"Look, Denny, I don't mean to be rude, but this is classified information. Don't you have errands to run or something?"

"I just finished one for Mr. Stosch. That's why I was next door. I couldn't be so close without popping in to see if you needed anything."

Jasper paused in front of his apartment door and clicked the key in the lock. "I do need something."

Denny's brown eyes lit up. "Sure! What can I do for you?"

"Leave me alone."

He yanked open the door, passed through, and would have shut it just as quick if the boy hadn't lodged his shoe in the doorframe. "Can't do that, detective. You need me."

"I? Need you?" Jasper coughed in an attempt to hold back laughter.

"Sure. You can't solve the cases without me."

Amused, Jasper clasped his hands behind him to play along. "Pray tell, why would a detective need a nosy errand boy to solve a crime?"

By Amber Schamel

"I'm smart—you know that. And fast. I can get information, run errands, sweet talk records out of the pretty lady in the employment department, and I scurry all over town. So I could keep tabs on a lot of things. An incognito informant, if you will."

Jasper bit his lip. How old was this kid? Seventeen? He'd been reading too many of those ridiculous Doyle novels, that's what. Well, he had to admit the boy was creative.

"Besides, every good detective needs a sidekick. What would Sherlock Holmes be without Watson? And, face it, what other choices do you have?"

"Nice try, kid. Get back to work." He flipped Denny a quarter and shut the door. He waited to hear the boy's tread fade away, but the shadow under the door didn't move.

"Okay, we'll talk later." Denny's voice muffled through beyond the door. "I'm sure you need some time to think it over."

After another moment, the boy trudged away. Jasper let out a breath and locked the door. He shrugged out of his overcoat and hung it on the tree. After Denny's interlude, he could finally unload his mind to his Council of Mirrors.

As his thoughts returned to Mr. Rudin, his stomach roiled. The deadly determination in the man's kindly eyes tossed him like a wayward vessel. He bowed his head and braced against the wall.

"Dear God, please help me stop him."

Leaving the cramped kitchen, he stepped into the small sitting area. He'd kept the furnishings sparse to give it the roomiest feel possible. A single chair and a side table—an invention of his own—that folded out to create a desk over the chair, and a lamp scarcely cluttered the space. The only wall hangings were his three beloved mirrors on each of the three windowless walls. He stood in the middle of the brown circular rug and faced the mirror on the left wall. He straightened its ornate gold frame, ignoring his thick upper lip made more idiotic by his slight overbite. How the features of his appearance aggravated him.

The mirror hung on the center wall was flawlessly straight with its plain, wooden frame. He gave his reflection half a smile. Now his large ears…there was a feature he could be proud of. They may rival a hound dog's in size, but also in perception.

Reaching out, he corrected the angle of the third mirror to the perfectly crooked slant he'd calculated. The warped posture accentuated the dark and gloomy frame, making it villainous. To him, each mirror held its own personality and insight.

"Where to begin?" He stared into the plain mirror. Then the ornate, then back at the dark one.

No longer was he seeing his face reflected, but a sickly image of Mr. Rudin. Dark circles encased his deep-set eyes, matching the frame's sooty shade.

"My life is not worth living." Mr. Rudin's dark thoughts swirled like smoke along the mirror's smooth surface. "Death will bring relief."

Jasper clenched his jaw. "What could possibly cause these dark thoughts? And how do I combat them?"

He crossed his arms and rubbed his chin. "Mr. Rudin is a wealthy man with a large house, social standing, good food—

By Amber Schamel

nearly anything he could wish. What would cause him to not want to live?"

"Money can't make one happy." The cloudy figure in the dark mirror spoke again. "Is this what men think it is to be rich? They've no idea. Superfluous, stressful, and meaningless."

Jerking to the left, Jasper stared into the golden mirror. "No, I am asking the wrong question, aren't I? Rather than why does he not want to live, I should be asking, what would make him *want* to live."

He needed a simple answer, so he stared straight ahead at the plain mirror and contemplated. What caused men to want to live?

Purpose. Mr. Rudin needed a purpose in his life. That was it.

Jasper nodded. So did all three of his duplicates. "Well then, we have a starting place. Let's formulate a plan."

A strand of dark hair fell across his eye. He blew it back. If anyone of the outside world saw him before his council, they'd admit him to a madhouse. Oh well. What worked, worked.

The cup of pencils turned over as he reached for it, sending the utensils scattering to the floor. So much for hoping he would lose his adolescent clumsiness. He straightened his vest before bending to pick them up. Grasping one firmly lest it escape again, he pressed it to the paper, drawing big shaky letters across the top.

PURPOSE.

He rubbed the pencil between his fingers. If he could show Mr. Rudin that his life had accomplished something, that he'd made a footprint on the earth, perhaps it would do the trick.

By Amber Schamel

FAMILY.

Mr. Rudin had a wife and a daughter. He would interview them for statements. Both of them owed their current existence to the man.

EMPLOYEES.

Surely, he could get some statements and testimonies from a few of them. If they hadn't been employed by the good man, how would they survive? And Mr. Rudin was known for his acts of kindness to people in need.

CHARITY.

Surely, the man had donated some funds that made a difference somehow. Another lead anyway.

Finally, at the bottom of his sheet of paper, he wrote two letters.

ME.

How much he could say about Mr. Rudin. He still remembered the rasp of his mother's voice on her deathbed. "I could never repay you, Gustov. You've been a brother, a friend, and a godsend." She couldn't have said it better. With a shiver, Jasper realized he owed everything to Mr. Rudin. And he would give everything within him to save the man.

Ouch. He shouldn't bite on his cheek so hard.

The wind howled outside his window. He crossed the room and pulled back the curtain. Must be near lunchtime with so many people in the streets. The sky had darkened, but it couldn't seem to decide whether to spit rain or snow. Jasper reached out and fingered the glass. Judging by the temperature, it would be freezing snow before long. Dash it. This storm had better not interfere with his ability to progress these cases.

He jerked the chain, clicking on the table lamp. The glow shone through the mosaic shade, casting cheery yellow and green reflections around the small room. The piece had been a housewarming gift from Mr. Rudin when he'd moved into the apartment almost a year ago. Jasper bowed his head and rested his palms against the small desk.

"God, I need your help. I can't handle this case on my own." He looked up, his reflection gazing back from the plain frame. "This isn't even a real case. How did I get sucked into this?"

He unbuttoned his shirtsleeves and rolled them up to his elbows. At least he had some sort of plan. Now to piece together the clues on the lab break-in. A real case could be solved.

Who would care for anything in the lab? Perhaps one of the employees. But why? Enemies? Mr. Rudin didn't have any.

This wasn't going very well. He could have some lunch. Who was he kidding? He could never eat when concentrating on a case. Water. Yes, that's what he needed. A good glass of water would help him think better.

In the kitchen, he poured a glass. While he sipped the cool liquid, his gaze fell upon the newspaper slid beneath his door. He picked it up and scanned the headlines.

IWW CASES FILL DOCKETS. IWW STRIKES CONTINUE.

Jasper clenched his jaw so hard pain lanced down his neck. Wobblies. The violent, mutinous rats. How much would he wager they had something to do with this? They seemed to be the source of everything troublesome in Denver these days.

He slapped the newspaper on the table and stomped back to

29

By Amber Schamel

his mirrors. Mr. Rudin's was one of the largest un-unionized factories in Denver. A prime target for militant unionists. They'd bring the city to its knees if someone didn't stop them. They stirred up the people, created havoc in the streets, but worst of all, they clogged the judicial system. With the courts so full of worthless "free speech" cases and the jails so full of Wobblies, real criminals were left roaming the streets. In Jasper's book, that made them the real criminals.

Pushing his hair back with one hand, he glared into the mirror. "Now, Jasper boy, don't put the Wobblies at the top of your suspect list just because you despise them."

Good advice. But who else did he have? No one.

With a snap of his fingers, he spun toward the door. "Then we follow this lead until we find a new scent."

By Amber Schamel

Chapter Four

After snatching his coat from the tree, Jasper made his way out the door. The rain—or snow—or whatever it was had increased, soaking him by the time he hopped on the streetcar. He cupped his hands and blew into them. Before he reached the factory, the chill had settled into his bones. He entered the building and veered left toward the employment department.

At the small reception area, he nodded at a young man wringing his hands as waited for his turn in the conference room. Jasper peeled off his overcoat and draped it on a chair.

"Afternoon, Hollock." The "pretty lady", as Denny had called her, didn't glance up from her paperwork. Her dark hair, pulled into a tidy bun at the nape of her neck, matched the brows arching intelligently above downcast eyes.

"Miss Leslie." He cleared his throat, trying to remember what he'd wanted to ask. Ah yes. "I would like to review some information on current employees."

By Amber Schamel

"How nice."

Jasper huffed and clasped his hands behind his back. He wouldn't take such obstinacy from anyone else. Why then, did he tolerate it from her? "Miss Leslie, would you be so kind as to provide me with the files for all employees currently working in the lab?"

She looked up, the golden specks in her hazel eyes glinting. "All of them? Hollock, do you think I have nothing else to do but succumb to your every curiosity?"

The tips of his ears grew hot. "Do you think I have the time to pester insignificant secretaries for useless information? I never clutter my mind with such." He jabbed a finger in her direction. "And that is Detective Hollock to you."

Miss Leslie had the most infuriating way of rolling her eyes and the pencil between her fingers at the same second. "And the files you left wreckage of last week, *detective*?"

Oh, the way she drawled the last word. He straightened and tugged his vest. "That is classified information I am not permitted to expose to level-one employees."

"The employee files are classified information as well, Sir Arrogant. Do you have clearance from Mr. Rudin to access these files?"

"Of course not." He wiped spittle from his lip. "To think I would require clearance from Mr. Rudin. I wished not to alarm him until I have more to go on."

She shrugged. "Well, this insignificant, level-one employee has a lot of honest work to do." She stood, smoothing the folds of her full, gray skirt. "Kindly take your scheming elsewhere.

Mr. Tucker, we are ready for you now." Stepping around Jasper, she led the young man into the next room.

Jasper drummed his fingers on her desk as he waited for her to return. Such insolence. He clenched his jaw while her heeled boots clicked back to her desk. "Now, really, Miss Leslie, can we get on with business? I need to see those files."

She sat, picked up her pencil, and continued with the ledger in front of her.

The clock on the wall ticked.

"Miss Leslie…?"

She gathered up several papers, tapped them on the desk, and crossed to a file cabinet.

Finally.

Jerking open the drawer, she fingered through it, dropped the papers inside, shoved it closed with a dramatic thud, and returned to her desk, all the while avoiding Jasper's glare.

This was too much. He slammed his fist on her desk. "Miss Leslie, if you don't get me those files this instant I will—I will—"

Her piercing gaze and delicate eyebrows lifted. "You will…?"

"I give you to the count of three, or I will march straight up to Mr. Rudin and demand you be—"

"There you are, detective," Denny bellowed from across the room. "I've been looking for you." In three short strides, the lad stood before him with a grin stretched across his face. He smiled a little wider when he turned to the infuriating "pretty" woman, revealing his dimple. "Why, hello, Bet. How are you? Have any

By Amber Schamel

errands for me today?"

Miss Leslie's eyes softened, and her mouth even curled up to return the boy's smile, making her look, well, almost pretty. "Denny, I was hoping you'd stop by. I do have a stack of letters I need to go out and a telegram needing sending."

Denny gave a bow, waving his hand with a flourish. "At your service, madam. Just as soon as I deliver this message to Detective Hollock, here." He shifted back to Jasper and frowned. "Is there something wrong, detective? You seem a bit ruffled."

Ruffled? Ha! He was doing well not to give the woman on the opposite side of the desk a swift escort to the door and a kick to help her along.

"Denny, my boy, I'd like you to take a good look at this creature." A smile crept across Jasper's face as he swept an arm toward Miss Leslie. "For here, you have the exotic breed of female troll descended from the Cyclops that taunted ancient civilizations. They are best identified by the upturned nose and aura of pride that reeks like rotting tomatoes. If you can, avoid them at all costs. In my line of work, however, one is often called upon to face the most treacherous beings known to man, such as this one."

The green tints in Miss Leslie's eyes darkened as her eyes swirled. For a moment, Jasper was certain his description of troll matched her perfectly. "Women only become trolls when they must rise to the occasion." She shifted her gaze to Denny. "Although, I can't hold a candle to the talent of your friend here."

The boy stood for a moment, his eyes wide, until he burst

By Amber Schamel

into laughter. "The two of you make quite a pair. You should go on stage together. You'd make millions." He laughed again, wiping a tear from the edge of one eye. "So, what's this all about?"

"I made a polite request for information, and Miss Leslie seems to think she has the authority to bar me from it." Jasper folded his arms and leveled his glare at the pig-headed secretary.

"Why, that can't be true. Bet has always been such a kind and helpful lady in all my experience, detective. She's my favorite person to run errands for simply because she is so cheerful."

Miss Leslie's face melted into a smile.

"See there, who wouldn't move Pike's Peak for such a lovely smile?" Denny picked up the letters and the telegram slip and shoved them into his leather satchel. "There must be some misunderstanding. Just what information are you looking for, detective?"

"A few employee files."

"Ah, of course." Swiping his cap from his head, Denny leaned across the desk and lowered his voice. "Do you know, Detective Hollock has hunted up a horrible threat to the factory? He's in the process of ferreting out the culprit, and it's ever so important. I'd love to tell you more details, Bet, but that's all we're permitted to say now. Do you think you could help us solve the case by bringing out a few files for us to peruse? If it's too much trouble, I suppose we could—"

"No, no, Denny. It's not too much trouble. I'd be happy to help. But do me a favor and teach your detective friend a few of

By Amber Schamel

your manners." She slid back her chair and crossed to the file cabinet. "Lab employees?"

Unbelievable. Jasper's glare shifted to the errand boy. Did the brat always get what he wanted?

Denny quirked a brow.

"Oh, uh, yes." Denny's elbow met his ribs. "Please."

With a smug grin, Miss Leslie returned carrying the files and held them out. Jasper reached for them, but she pulled back, her brows rising.

He forced a smile. "Thank you, Miss Leslie."

She plopped the files into his waiting arms and started for the interview room. "Don't make a mess of them, or you'll be banned for life, Hollock."

He chomped down hard on his tongue. The metallic taste of blood filled his mouth, but it was better than opening it again.

After she disappeared, he faced Denny. The boy gave a shrug. "I told you. You need me."

"Hmmph." Jasper hefted the files and headed for Mr. Rudin's conference room. "Bet? Just what kind of term is that?"

Denny matched his pace. "Her name is Elizabeth. Her niece calls her Bet, so I picked it up. She thinks it's cute."

It would be cute. If she weren't so insufferable.

"So, what do you say? We make quite the team, don't ya think?"

Jasper halted, his free hand curling at his side. He was not in the mood for pestering. "Deliver the telegram, Denny."

"Right. I'd better get these out before they close. I'll catch up with you later, boss."

"Denny." Jasper's call caught the boy before he rounded the corner. "Don't call me 'boss'."

A mischievous grin, and the lad was gone. At least Jasper had a few moments of peace to gain some clues out of these files. Heaving the load under his right arm, he opened the conference room door then spread them across the table.

He eased into a chair and rubbed his temples. Surely, the files would give him a hint at a motive for the break-in. One of the lab employees must have ties to the Wobblies. But how could they? Jasper had done extensive background checks on each employee before Mr. Rudin's decision to hire.

He flipped open the first file and sifted through the contents. He remembered each of them as soon as he read their name. He'd checked out their former employment, scouted out their housing districts, even spoke to their families. Especially in-laws. In-laws usually told any secrets people tried to hide.

After several hours of poring over the files, he slammed the last one shut and closed his weary eyes. They had to be bloodshot after staring at scribbled notes and fine print. And still no leads.

Think, Hollock.

The intruder either came in through the window or had a key. The window...could be almost anyone. The key narrowed it to three people, Charlie, Kendall, and—Mr. Rudin. Of course! Why hadn't he thought to ask in the first place? Mr. Rudin had been at the factory nearly all night. Perhaps he entered the lab for some reason, and all this fuss was over nothing.

Jasper exhaled and opened his eyes. Denny, arms crossed

By Amber Schamel

and leaning on the table, stared at him. "Any clues?"

Clearing his throat, Jasper stood and tugged his vest back into place. "No."

"You were thinking about something else then. I saw a grin before you opened your eyes." Mischief sparkled in the boy's eyes. "You were thinking of your girlfriend, weren't you?"

He shot Denny a glare. "There are other things to smile about, you know."

Denny quirked a brow. "She's pretty, isn't she?"

"Don't be ridiculous. I was not thinking of any such thing. I'd simply remembered something I hadn't thought of before that may solve this whole case."

The lad's smile faded. "Are cases the only thing that makes you happy?"

Lifting one shoulder, Jasper glanced toward the ceiling. "Quite possibly, yes."

"That's why you're going to be the best detective in the history of Denver." Denny punched his arm. "What'd you remember?"

"I need to speak with Mr. Rudin. He was in the factory late into the night and may have been our so-called intruder."

Denny's head jerked back. "Ol' Mr. Rudin? How boring."

"Let's hope so. Come on."

Did he just invite the kid to go with him? His jolly mood must be getting the best of him. "On second thought, maybe it would be best if you returned these files to Miss Leslie. She'd be glad to take them from you."

With a sigh, Denny scuffed mud from his shoe into the rug.

By Amber Schamel

"Aw, one of these days I'm not going to be an errand boy anymore." He picked up the files and jaunted toward the employment department.

Jasper was all too happy to head in the opposite direction. Although, Miss Leslie was at least more pleasing to look at than Mr. Stosch. However similar their temperaments.

By Amber Schamel

By Amber Schamel

Chapter Five

Mr. Stosch was absent, so Jasper tapped on Mr. Rudin's door.

"Yes?"

Easing the door open, he poked his head inside. His employer stood before the window, gazing to the street below. The posture made Jasper nervous, given his mentor's state of mind. "Good evening, sir."

"Jasper, I expected you would be headed home by now. It's snowing, you know."

That statement wasn't reassuring, either. "Yes, well, sir, I had a few things to look into first. I wondered if you might have seen the lab recently."

Mr. Rudin's white brows dipped as he turned and focused his full attention on Jasper. "The lab? No. Is there some reason I should?"

"Not particularly, I just thought you might like to see how

By Amber Schamel

they're getting along. I know businessmen like yourself often like to stop in unannounced to see how the manager handles things." Jasper took a few casual steps into the room and clasped his hands behind him, hoping to appear nonchalant. He never was very good at that.

"Are you unhappy with the manager's performance? Has he done something to arouse your suspicions?"

"Suspicious? No, sir. What reason would I have to be suspicious?"

Mr. Rudin's arms folded across his ample form. "You're lying. Your eye is twitching. It always does when there's something you should tell me."

Dash it. The old man knew him too well. But he couldn't divulge his suspicions. Not yet.

"Hello, Mr. Rudin, I've a note for you from the employment department." Denny swept into the room, pulled off his cap, and extended his hand.

Thank You, God.

Mr. Rudin accepted the note and glanced over the contents. "Good. Tell Miss Leslie nine o'clock will be fine." He returned the paper and refocused on Jasper. "Looks like we have another chap for you to stalk, detective."

"Please, Mr. Rudin, you know I don't stalk your potential employees."

The man's dark eyes twinkled. He crossed to his desk and held out his candy bowl to Denny. "Here, have one of these. They're very good. Made with Rudin sugar, wouldn't you know."

By Amber Schamel

Denny took one, popped it in his mouth, and closed his eyes. "Like a piece of heaven, Mr. Rudin."

A flatterer for certain. But that could be a good trait if properly channeled. Jasper waved away the offered candies and walked to the window. "You are spot on, sir. Time to be making our way home before the snow gets worse. Will you be going soon?"

Mr. Rudin let out a long breath and plopped into his leather chair. "I suppose so."

Hmm. He'd better look into Mr. Rudin's family affairs. Perhaps something there motivated his dismal thoughts.

"All right then, goodnight, sir."

The old man's eyes had misted over, and he seemed far away. "Yes, goodnight."

Jasper jerked his head toward the door, motioning Denny to follow. He left the office door slightly ajar, hoping the lack of privacy would keep Mr. Rudin from doing anything rash.

"This isn't the way out," Denny said to his back. "Where are we going?"

"I want to take a turn around the factory. Just to make sure everything is as it should be before we leave."

"This is why you're the detective, and I'm the sidekick."

Jasper stopped. Denny slammed into his back. "You are not my sidekick. It's just me. Alone."

"Even Jesus had disciples."

"Yes. And they crucified Him."

Moving again, Jasper lengthened his strides. The lab was tightly locked, and no one lingered in the hallways nor in the

By Amber Schamel

other offices as he checked them one by one. Miss Leslie had gone home, though her office still smelled of lilacs. The pulp warehouse was empty as were the boiling rooms.

"This factory is kinda creepy when it's so quiet." Denny's voice echoed through the Crystallization Room.

Jasper held a finger to his lips before proceeding down the metal staircase. If anyone was loitering around, he didn't want to announce their coming.

They rounded the enormous machine, their shoes clacking on the concrete, when Jasper came to a halt. Something was amiss. A cloth sack was tossed aside, and a hatch was open on the crystallizer. He glanced around, searching for signs of recent occupation. The room was still as a graveyard. Well, besides Denny's gasp from behind.

"Has someone been in here?"

"Don't touch anything." Jasper twisted and caught the boy's gaze. "You hear?"

"Sure, boss."

Too concerned to be annoyed, Jasper ignored the comment and picked up the sack. Little wisps fell like fairy dust as he did so.

"Is that…hair?" Denny's nose wrinkled.

"Human hair." Jasper turned the sack over. No printing. Just a plain white sack. His gut clenched as he stepped toward the open hatch. Several strands of short hair rested on the lip.

This was bad.

"Denny, find the janitor. If he's still around, bring him here at once."

The boy scurried away without a word. Jasper's gaze drifted over the giant machine, then dropped to the floor. Something shiny protruded from beneath. He bent, expecting to find a forgotten nickel, but a key emerged. RSF engraved one side.

He rubbed his fingers together. Rudin Sugar Factory? Could it be an employee's key? Why would one of the workers possess one? And how many doors would it open?

The lab?

"I found him, boss." Denny came trotting toward him, panting as he waved the janitor onward.

"Charlie, do you know how to open this machine?"

"Sure, detective." He huffed a strand of graying hair out of his eyes. "But why?"

"Someone has sabotaged this machine." Jasper held up the sack. "Please open it at once."

The janitor pulled keys from his pocket.

"Wait." Jasper reached for Charlie's ring of keys. "Which is the key to this room?"

Charlie shrugged. "I only have a master key, not one to this specific room."

"Fine, which is that?"

The janitor's grimy finger picked a steel key out of the bunch. Jasper held the key he'd found beneath the machine against it. A perfect match, except one was slightly longer.

Jasper shoved the keys back at Charlie. "All right, get this thing open."

Charlie made quick work of opening the main compartment. Jasper peeked inside. Hair clung with static around the top of the dome and combined with the gooey mixture at the bottom in a mortared mess.

Just as he suspected. Complete contamination.

If this got out, if the newspapers got word, if the Wobblies…this would be disastrous. Rudin Sugar would have a hard time salvaging their reputation and not losing massive amounts of business. The Wobblies would exploit the incident. Anything to damage a nonunion company.

Jasper's fingernails dug half-moon shapes into his palms. He had to stop it.

Chapter Six

Jasper's exhaustion tripled as he slogged through the wet snow. It had taken hours for Charlie to get the hair cleaned out. But at least no one else would know of the incident. He'd threatened Denny with jail if he opened his mouth, and Charlie was all too happy to keep quiet for an extra dollar. But with this new development, Jasper could no longer keep the threat from Mr. Rudin. Divulging the issue would make things worse. Well, the man hadn't stayed at the factory again tonight. That was hopeful.

By the time Jasper approached Montgomery Court, the paperboy was unloading stacks of the latest printing at the corner. He tipped his cap as Jasper passed. "Morning, sir."

Was it really morning already? He glanced at the stack of newspapers. Sure enough, the date was December 2, and already they were touting the news of some contamination of—

Skidding to a stop, Jasper nearly fell to the icy walk. He

47

scrambled to keep his balance, bracing himself on the brick building for support.

"Are you all right, sir?" The paperboy's eyes hadn't been so wide a moment ago.

Standing at the wall, Jasper allowed a few pants before inching back toward the corner. "Let me see those." He dug in his pocket for a nickel and dropped it in the boy's hand.

SUGAR FACTORY CONTAMINATED! HAIR FOUND IN GOODS AT RUDIN SUGAR FACTORY.

Jasper coughed. How? The perpetrator must have gone directly to the press. Would an angry employee do such a thing? Perhaps. But more likely someone else. Someone who knew the press game. Someone like the Wobblies.

He trudged up to his apartment. He would find out who was behind this article as soon as the newspaper office opened. For now, he needed sleep.

*****

Jasper gulped down the rest of his black coffee and plunked his head down on the kitchen table. With his mind running in circles over this case, sleep had been as obstinate as Miss Leslie. Then after he'd finally dozed off, images of Mr. Rudin twirling a pistol on his desk haunted his dreams.

He lifted his head and gave it a good shake. *Keep your mind focused, Hollock.*

The key was his best clue. Being a master narrowed down suspects to those possessing one. Charlie did, obviously, but his was still on his ring. Kendall had a lab key, but not a master. Who else?

A knock rattled his door. He dragged himself from the chair and flicked the lock.

"I didn't say a peep, boss." Denny clutched a newspaper to his chest. "I give my word."

"I know, kid. The perpetrator must have done it. I saw the paper on my way home last night. Neither you nor Charlie would have had time to get the word to the paper."

"Well, you better perk up and come quick. Mr. Rudin wants to speak with you."

"I imagine he does." Jasper exhaled. "Let me grab my coat."

Lord, help me. I've not progressed with Rudin's first issue, and now I have to make another.

He followed Denny to the street where the boy stopped to strap on a pair of skis. Jasper raised a brow. "Do those things really work?"

"Of course, they do. I'll be dashing through the snow like a one-horse open sleigh." Denny laughed and pushed off with a couple sticks. "Race you to the factory?"

Jasper took a step. But his shoe slipped on a patch of ice, and his backside whacked the ground. Wet cold instantly seeped through his trousers. Dash it. This was going to be an enjoyable day.

When Jasper slogged into the factory, Mr. Stosch crossed his arms and chuckled as Jasper brisked past him. "Weather not to your liking, detective? You could have wiped the snow from your back before tramping up here."

Ignoring him, Jasper threw open the door to Mr. Rudin's office. "Mr. Rudin?"

By Amber Schamel

A thump sounded beneath the giant desk. "Oy."

"Mr. Rudin!" Jasper's heart skipped a beat as he rushed around the desk. *God, don't let me be too late.*

His employer was down on all fours, backing out from under the desk.

"Sir, are you all right?"

"Dah." He sat up and rubbed the crown of his head, disheveling his white hair. "I was looking for my key. It has gone missing."

One of Jasper's brows ticked. "Which key, specifically, sir?"

"My master key opens every door in the factory. I keep it in that drawer there." He pointed to a tiny drawer tucked into the underside of the desk. "But it's gone."

Jasper padded his breast pocket and pulled out the key he'd discovered. "Did it look like this?"

Mr. Rudin's snowy brows scrunched together as he took the key and held it close to his nose. "This is it, all right. How did you end up with it?"

One part of the mystery solved, anyway. "I found it at the scene last night."

His employer stood, bracing himself on the desk as his aging legs adjusted. "Scene? Does it have to do with this?" His knuckle rapped the newspaper on his desk. "How does an article about the contamination of my factory hit the paper without me knowing?"

Biting his lip, Jasper rocked back on his heels. "I was hoping it wouldn't be serious enough to alert you, that my hunch would prove wrong."

By Amber Schamel

"What hunch? Get to the point. I knew last night you weren't telling me something, but I demand you spill it now." Mr. Rudin waved at the leather chair opposite his desk. "Sit down."

Jasper obeyed and waited for Mr. Rudin to settle into his chair as well. "Yesterday morning, the janitor alerted me to the fact that the lab door was found ajar. I inspected the room, but as far as we can tell, nothing was stolen. I thought perhaps it had been you checking in on things, and we had nothing to fret about. After you denied it, I decided to take a turn about the factory once everyone left. Just to ensure everything was in order. That's when I discovered a sack in the Crystallization Room. Someone had brought it in and deposited its contents into the machine. Whoever it was must have heard us coming and fled. Must have gone straight for the newspaper office, too. I called Charlie in to clean it up. We were here half the night to see to it."

"Atrocious. Who would do such a thing to old Rudin's sugar?" Mr. Rudin leaned back in his chair, his hands clenched into fists. "I never wanted to have enemies, Jasper. Why does everyone hate me?"

"Sir, there are many who love you. I personally haven't met a single person who hates you." Too bad Denny wasn't here. He'd do a better job at making the old man feel better.

"Now just look at this article. All my clients will refuse to buy my sugar. They'll take their business somewhere else, and I will be cheated out of every penny I've worked for all these years."

"Please, sir, don't get worked up. We'll correct this with

51

another article in tomorrow's edition about how it was a mistake or potentially a sabotage. Your clients will understand."

"Sabotage? Oh, my reputation is ruined. Just like everything else. I don't want to die penniless. I'll shoot myself before they can take it from me."

His wrinkly hands shaking, Mr. Rudin jerked open a drawer and rummaged through it.

Jasper jumped up and caught his wrist. "No, Mr. Rudin, please. No need for that. I won't let these people take your business. We'll get to the bottom of it, but I need your help if we are to succeed."

"How am I a help? It seems every problem comes back 'round to me. Everything I touch turns into a muddle."

Jasper crossed to the drink bar and poured his employer a glass of brandy. "Here now, perhaps this will calm you." He pressed the glass into Mr. Rudin's hand.

Thankfully, the old man downed it. He relaxed, his breaths heavy gasps ruffling his white mustache.

"That's it, sir. We'll get the facts and this whole situation ironed out just fine." Jasper settled back in the chair, watching every tick of Mr. Rudin's jaw. He needed to gain the man's insight, but he couldn't get far with him in the midst of a conniption fit. "I don't think you understand what your life has meant to me."

Rudin's eyes rose to meet his.

"I was too young to remember, but my mother told me many times about the first night she met you and your wife. She was so terrified that somehow she'd be tracked from Chicago and my

52

father's murderer would finish us both. She feared that till the day she died. But when you took her hand during those last few, ragged breaths, when you assured her I would have a place here at the company, all fear left her eyes in a single tear that coursed down her jaw. Do you remember?"

Mr. Rudin stared at nothing as if a trance had fallen over him. "I wiped it away."

"Yes, and with it, every fear my dear mother harbored for twenty years."

"She smiled then. Like she was glimpsing an angel."

Jasper leaned forward and touched the man's hand. "I believe she was."

"I never had a baby sister. But your mother brought such joy to our house, as if she was what I never had." With a sigh, he withdrew his hand and pursed his lips. "But she's gone now. You and I are left with the problems and ugliness of the world."

"Yes, sir, but amidst all the darkness and ugliness, your kindness to me and my mother stands as a candle burning in a window. Don't snuff it out."

Mr. Rudin stood with a grunt. "So, who broke into my factory, Jasper? An employee?"

"I had thought so initially, but anyone could have come in through the lab window. Anyone with knowledge about the refining process could have brought in contaminants."

"What about the key? How would they take it from my office without knowing where to find it?"

Rubbing his chin, Jasper eyed the door. It was cracked open. Hadn't he closed it behind him? He tiptoed over and jerked it open to Mr. Stosch standing at a filing cabinet next to the door, one wrinkled hand hovering over the drawer.

Jasper's eyes narrowed. "No newspaper to keep you busy, Mr. Stosch?"

The secretary tilted his chin upward and sniffed. "I have plenty on my list today, detective. So don't be asking any favors." He strode to his desk and sat.

Jasper clicked the door closed and switched the lock. He approached his employer and lowered his voice. "Has Mr. Stosch given you any reason to suspect him of ill will?"

"Stosch? Why no. He's as great a fellow as any could ask for."

Somehow, Jasper doubted the description. "Who else would know where your key is?"

"Not Stosch." Rudin's expression fell. "Let it be anyone but him." He covered his face with his hands, muffling his words. "Can't I trust anyone?"

Taking a deep breath, Jasper gulped down his frustration. Did he have to cast a shadow of doom over everything? How would he ever get the man to see a reason for living when all he could see was hopeless?

"Well, perhaps the thief simply snooped until he found it." Not likely. The thief would've had to be expertly quick given the space of time between Mr. Rudin's departure and Jasper's discovery—less ten minutes. "But, Mr. Rudin, does anyone else possibly know where you kept the key?"

"I don't know. Perhaps someone observed me taking it out at some point."

Jasper gave a nod. He wasn't gaining any ground here. He strolled to the window and looked out. It would be difficult for someone to see from the street into his second-story office. "I hate to ask, sir, but can you think of anyone who would have a reason to threaten your business?"

The man was quiet for several moments, twirling his mustache around one finger. "Not living, anyway."

Jasper turned. "Not living?"

Rudin gave him a weak smile. "Never mind. Let the dead rest, shall we? No need to dig up what's been buried."

Maybe. But burying something alive never worked out, and it sounded like this issue wasn't as dead as Mr. Rudin wanted it to be.

Mr. Rudin folded his fingers into a steeple. "So, what do we do now?"

"First, the newspaper. I'm going down there to find out who was behind that article, and I will make them run another story to expose the facts, while not yet exposing our suspicions."

A hint of the old sparkle returned to Mr. Rudin's eyes. "I'm glad that's your job, not mine."

No fooling. Right now Jasper was wishing he did have a "sidekick" to handle some of these tasks. But he'd need someone more experienced than a seventeen-year-old errand boy. "In the meantime, I will continue to search for any ties to the Wobblies."

Especially concerning Mr. Stosch.

Besides all that, Jasper desperately needed to make a call on Mrs. Rudin and get some answers before her husband decided to leave her running the factory. He pivoted toward the door. "Do let me know if you remember anything else of importance, sir."

*****

Jasper yanked the door open and entered the newspaper office, a copy of the article under his arm. He slapped the paper on the receptionist's desk and pinned it with his finger. "Detective Jasper Hollock of Rudin Sugar Company. I need to speak with the reporter responsible for this article immediately."

The girl's eyes widened as she leaned forward to read the headline. "Oh…" She swallowed, her eyes darting over her left shoulder.

"First door on the right?" Clenching the paper, he started in that direction.

"W–wait. He can't see anyone without an appointment."

"He'll make an exception, miss. This is an emergency." He threw open the door, startling a heavyset man with his feet propped up on the desk. His surprise threw him off-kilter, and he toppled backward, disappearing from Jasper's sight with a thud.

Papers, some held down with iron horseshoes or golf club heads, piled high atop his desk, ready to avalanche the brass nameplate reading Alan McCracken. A portrait of Shakespeare clung cockeyed to the white wall behind him.

McCracken scrambled to his feet, his plump face growing redder. "Who in Drake's crew are you? You can't just storm into my office."

Jasper dipped a bow, waving the newspaper article like a royal fan. "Detective Hollock of Rudin Sugar Company, at your service." He slammed the paper atop the rubble. "Are you the author of this article?"

The flush drained from the reporter's face. "I—uh—well…"

His receptionist lingered outside the doorway. "I'm sorry, Alan. I tried to stop him."

Alan straightened and, with a sniff, leveled his gaze at Jasper. "Yes, I am. What can I do for you, detective?"

"Where did you get this information?"

The reporter tugged at his sleeves and righted his chair. "My sources are confidential." Snatching his pen from the desk, he replaced the cap.

"Confidential? Perhaps. Reliable? Not a chance." Jasper looked closer and braced his hands on the desk. "What kind of intelligent reporter publishes a report of a contamination without contacting the factory where the supposed incident took place?"

The pen dropped from McCraken's ink-stained fingers. "My job is to report facts quickly."

"Quite so. Facts. Tell me then, Mr. Expert Reporter, what time did this said incident occur?" Jasper lifted his brows awaiting an answer.

"Sometime y–yesterday. Evening. The exact time is not important."

"How much sugar was affected? What was done with it? How did the contamination occur?"

Rather than reply, McCracken raised his beefy thumb and chewed the nail.

Jasper pointed to the chair. "Sit down." The chair creaked as the reporter plopped down. "Now, Mr. McCracken, be very helpful and cooperative, and I may reconsider my decision to

57

report you to the sheriff for fraud, slander, and exploitation."

"Fine. I'll tell you what I know."

"Which doesn't appear to be much, but will be a start." Jasper pulled a notepad and pencil out of his coat pocket. "Where did you get the information?"

"A message was delivered to my office. The message contained the information published in the article."

"Do you still have it?"

McCracken surveyed his mountains of paper. "Um…somewhere."

Jasper sighed. "Never mind. Did the person sign the message? Who was it from?"

"The *anonymous* tip claimed it would be all over the place if we didn't get it to print quick."

"Details, people. Details." Jasper's pencil dulled with each tap on the page. "Did it give any indication as to how they came about the information? Did it sound like the informant may have been an employee of the factory?"

"It only gave facts, but did mention how the factory would probably wish to hide the instance."

This was going to take a while. Jasper stepped into the hall, hooked two fingers around a chair's backrest, and swung the thing into the office. "How was the message delivered?"

"A post boy brought it in."

"You reporters claim to have supernatural intuition—did you get the hunch it was connected to the Wobblies?"

McCracken settled back in the chair and crossed his right leg over his knee. "Not really, but we have received anonymous tips

58

from their organization before."

Finally, something worth jotting down. "What kinds of tips have they given you?"

"Details on riots, injuries, information on court cases, a broad spectrum, really."

"And how were those delivered? Same post boy?"

McCracken frowned. "That'd be a question for the receptionist. I'm not exactly sure how it got here. All I know is that it did. Are you finished with your interrogation yet?"

"Not quite." Jasper leaned forward and tapped the article about Rudin Sugar. "About this, you need to write an apology admitting your false information and publish it in tomorrow's issue."

"What?" The reporter's round face flushed red again.

"You reported false information that threatens the company's reputation. Now you must own to it."

McCracken stood, picked up the issue, and tossed it in Jasper's lap. "Get out of my office."

"My pleasure." Jasper rose as well. "I need to drop by the police station and your competitor's office anyway. I'm sure they'll both be interested in the *details* of this scandal." He dragged the chair toward the door.

"Wait." McCracken ran a hand down one side of his face. "Are you saying there was no contamination whatsoever?"

"I'm saying you reported with no validated facts. That's what you need to correct."

A grin slid across his face. "So there was an incident." He fumbled in his desk for a notepad and snatched up a pen. "Was it really hair in the sugar?"

"I'll give you till tomorrow morning to retract your article. If it isn't there, I'm going to be your nightmare." Jasper continued toward the door. He hoped the scraping of the chair legs against the carpet added effect.

McCracken followed him, almost panting like a dog after a bone. "You suspect foul play, don't you? With no idea who it is."

Jasper spun around and dropped a business card into the reporter's breast pocket. "If you hear anything further from your anonymous contact, do let me know."

Chapter Seven

December 3, 1913

The snowstorm had eased, but a few flurries still drifted from the cloudy sky. Jasper squinted against the landscape's white brightness. He caught a trolley and headed for the Rudin mansion.

The trolley veered from street to street, rocking the commuters in a steady rhythm. A man with a briefcase stood up and began to sing at the top of his voice.

"Workers of the world, awaken!

Break your chains, demand your rights.

All the wealth you make is taken;

By exploiting parasites.

Shall you kneel in deep submission;

From your cradles to your graves?

Is the height of your ambition;

To be good and willing slaves?"

By Amber Schamel

Jasper elbowed the man next to him. "What do you think of these fellows?"

"I'd prefer a Christmas carol, but that one has a nice voice. I should recruit him for the theater."

"Is it a Union job?"

The man chuckled. Not a part of them, then. Still, he might have some insight to point Jasper in the right direction.

The singer ended his serenade and launched into a speech. Jasper leaned closer to the man beside him. "They're up to some interesting tactics. You think they'll gain any ground in Denver?"

"Seems to be. I have a cousin who goes to all their meetings."

"That so?"

"Sure. Tells me all about how they're going to be the savior of the working class."

"I see. Where do they intend to start?"

"The free speech fights were the start. Now I guess they just organize members, strikes, and the like."

"Do you know where they meet?"

"In the streets, I think."

Jasper lowered his voice another notch. "I've heard they're 'radical'. Do you think they'll turn to violence?"

The man scratched his bristly chin, bushy brows sinking. "Well, I don't think that's their intent, but you remember the trial of Bill Haywood. Most folks think he had more to do with setting off that bomb. With him as their leader, you never know what they'll do next." The man stood. "Well, this is my stop.

62

Nice talking with you."

Jasper nodded as the man exited the car. He sat back and folded his arms. He'd have to spy out a meeting and watch for any Rudin employees. One of them had to be tied to this case.

He hopped off the streetcar and sloshed to the Barnum subdivision. The Rudins' mansion dominated the top of a hill. Made of red brick with a nod at the Colonial era, castle-like towers guarded both sides of a spacious front porch. Wide white steps offset the red, and matching white trim and scattered windows provided a cheery look. Already the customary oversized wreath graced the front door. It wouldn't be long before the gigantic red Christmas bows dotted the railing.

How he'd enjoyed this house as a child, yet bittersweet memories always rose at the sight of it. His mouth went dry. He missed his mother. Loneliness swept over him like a drift of snow.

Determination quickened his pace. Mr. Rudin must live. Jasper would do whatever it took to ensure he did. He wouldn't lose him, too.

He trotted up the steps and rapped on the front door. A maid opened. "Detective Hollock, come on in. I'm sorry, but Mr. Rudin isn't home from the factory yet."

"Quite all right, Lena. I am here to see the missus, today. In the parlor?"

"Yes, sir." She took his coat, and he headed down the hall.

The parlor door was ajar. He tapped and poked his head inside. The flowery wallpaper and warmth of the room would fool you into thinking it was spring, if not for the half-decorated

63

tree in the corner. A rose-petal scent he always associated with Mrs. Rudin tickled his nostrils. Sure enough, she sat in her usual place. Poised like a queen upon the cream-colored divan sorting ornaments. "Afternoon, Mrs. Rudin."

"Jasper, what a pleasant surprise. What has kept you away so long?" The woman laid aside the box and met him halfway across the room, her high-waisted, mauve skirt swooshing around her ankles. A healthy blush brightened her so that, even with a few wrinkles, she retained a spirit of youth.

He clasped both her hands and gave one of those cheeks a peck. "Oh, you know how it is. Your husband taught me to work."

She laughed, but it was a hollow sound, not her typical infectious giggle.

After tea was ordered, Jasper motioned to the couch. "I wondered if I might ask you a bit about Mr. Rudin's life. I'm working on a new project, and I want to pen a record of his accomplishments."

"Well now, is he so famous that you hope to get rich off his biography?"

Smiling, Jasper winked. "Something like that." He pulled out his notepad. "When did you first meet him?"

She settled against the cushions, her pink lips bowing upward. "We were young then. Back in New York… His family had emigrated from Russia, you see, so he was the new boy in the neighborhood the year I turned sixteen. Charming as he was, every girl on the street was swooned by him. I was, too, but I was better at hiding it. I pretended not to notice him, and he

By Amber Schamel

accepted the challenge."

There was the giggle. Jasper grinned.

"The tactics he used to get me to speak to him! He'd been in the neighborhood about two weeks, and we still hadn't been introduced. I looked out my window one afternoon and saw him passing by my house. He took his wallet from his pocket and tossed it on my front porch, then just walked away. Of course, I had to return the wallet. A fair amount of bills were in it, too. I'll never forget the twinkle in his eye when he saw me standing on his porch, wallet in hand."

"Did he have a curly mustache then, too?"

"Goodness, no. He wasn't able to grow that until he was past thirty. But how proud he was when he finally could. He threatened to wear gold ornaments on the tips."

After a moment of laughter, she sighed. "What I would give to have my old Gustov back. He's not been himself as of late." She bowed her head, and a gray curl fell against her soft, white blouse. "In some ways, life is easier than when we were young. Just look at this house. But in others…age brings cares we didn't used to have."

Jasper reached over and patted her hand. "It will be all right. We'll find a way to get him back. Perhaps this narrative of his life will help."

She offered a weak smile. "Yes. Do go on, Jasper."

"If you met in New York, what brought you to Denver?"

"Gustov and I were deep in love, but our parents didn't approve of the match. There are some strange Russian customs, you know. So he and I eloped. That's when we came here."

By Amber Schamel

"So Mr. Rudin made his success without family aid or connections?"

"Well, away from family and without contact with them. Though we had a bit of money when we left. He used it as a start, but mostly his tenacity made him what he is."

Lena stepped through the door carrying a tray of tea. "Here you are, ma'am."

After noting these comments, Jasper set aside his notebook and claimed the steaming cup Mrs. Rudin offered. "I've always admired Mr. Rudin's kindness and generosity. He must have touched many people in the community."

"Indeed. He believes in sharing what we are gifted with. He's always been passionate about charity."

"If you don't mind me asking, would you name a few of the charities has he contributed to?"

"The Orthodox church, of course, and the orphanage have been our favorites. Gustov also does so much for the poorer parts of town and especially his employees, as I'm sure you know."

After a sip of tea, he set down the cup and scratched out those notes. He'd have to interview someone at the orphanage and one of the priests.

Now he needed to find a way to ask if she'd felt threatened at any point without alarming the dear woman. "I'm sure such a charitable reputation has created much goodwill in the community."

"Yes." She frowned and edged her teacup and saucer onto the tray before her. "Well, until recently. These union groups seem to be making Gustov out as a villain, only because he is the employer rather than employee."

"Have you felt a change in attitude since their formation?"

Her lips pursed into a thin line. "I've started sending Lena to do the shopping. A few people in town actually seem to...to *dislike* me. Sometimes they charge ridiculous prices far above what the item is marked."

"The organization claims you have nothing in common with the working class. They just need to see that you are a human the same as they are."

She nodded, but her teacup clattered against the saucer when she picked it up.

He swallowed, fearing the answer to his next question. "Have you had any disturbances lately?"

"Not particularly, though I suspected a man was following us for some time last month. Nothing came of it, thank goodness. I haven't seen him since."

He bit his lip. "What did he look like?"

"I couldn't say for certain. His hat was pulled down over his face, and his coat collar flipped up." She smoothed her skirt, and trouble clouded her eyes.

He cringed. He hadn't meant to make her uneasy. "How is Ana?"

Her face brightened at the mention of her daughter. "Oh, she's fine. That little grandson of mine will be two next Wednesday."

"I bet that youngster loves his grandfather."

Again, the smile disappeared. "He would, but unfortunately

By Amber Schamel

Ana and her husband are so busy…we rarely get to see him. They're into all the social circles, you know."

Something about her statement didn't sit right. How would a daughter not have time for her parents? Especially when she was the couple's only child?

"I sure have enjoyed visiting, Mrs. Rudin. But I do have to get going. Much to do before the sun goes down on me." They stood, and he wrapped one arm around her frail shoulders. "Forgive me. I will try to stop by more often."

Smiling, she laid a hand on his cheek. "I always love to see you, dear."

Leaving the Rudin mansion, Jasper took off toward the orphanage. It was only a few blocks down, situated in an old house built in Denver's early days. The shutters needed painting, but the brick structure appeared in good condition, considering.

A snowball whizzed past him and hit a tree in the yard. He stopped and looked around, but the only movement came from a branch at the edge of a shrub. He took another step, and another snowball slammed his back.

"Ow!" He whirled around as a boy ducked behind a tree. The snowball at his feet had split open to reveal a walnut-sized rock. He'd have a whelp come morning. He eyed the tree branches, laden with snow.

Jasper couldn't help a smirk as he bent and picked up the rock. He aimed and slung with all his might. The stone hit the intended branch, dumping an armload of snow.

The boy behind the tree screeched as snow pelted his head. *That'll show him.* Jasper faced the house, but he stopped as

By Amber Schamel

sobbing met his ears. Guilt smacked him over the head, and he winced.

He tiptoed through the snow and around the tree. A small boy about nine years of age sat covered in snow. His nose was red, and tears glistened on his cheeks.

"There, there, it's not so bad. You can't win every fight." Jasper waved a hand. "Come on then, shake it off and let's go inside."

The boy sobbed louder. "It's cold." He shifted, and one leg appeared from beneath the snow. Jasper's stomach twisted into a knot. Steel braces fastened the kid's left leg.

"I'm sorry, lad. Let me help you up." He stooped, gripped the boy under the arms, and stood him up. He swiped at the boy's shoulders, dusting off the snow. "Are you all right?"

"I think so." But when he took a step, he wavered.

Jasper reached out to steady him, but when he did, the boy fell into his arms. He swept him up and marched to the house. "Let's get you inside."

The boy trembled in his grip. "Why do I have to be different from all the other boys?" He buried his face in Jasper's coat, muffling his sobs.

As Jasper mounted the stairs, the front door flew open. "Oh, bless you, sir. Please bring him in and set him on the sofa." The matron ushered him into the parlor and fluffed the pillows behind the lad when he laid him down on a brown sofa. "Shhh, it's all right, Eddy."

Jasper knelt before the boy and wiped the tears from his cheeks. "Are you hurt?"

Eddy shook his head. "Just c–cold."

Snow caked Eddy's frozen shoelaces. The ice cut at Jasper's fingertips. Shaking loose mini snowballs, he managed to pry the laces off without upsetting the boy's leg. He shook open the blanket offered by the matron and tucked it around him. "Better?"

"Thank you, mister…?" Blue eyes blinked up at him.

"Hollock. Detective Hollock, actually." He extended a hand. "And you are Eddy, I presume?"

Those blue eyes widened. "Detective Hollock? Denny's boss?"

Jasper clenched his jaw and counted to ten. "I am a…uh…a friend of Denny's."

"He talks about you all the time. He says he's going to work with you, and together you'll save Denver from all the bad guys."

"Denny can tell good stories. You should tell him to write books."

"He reads a lot of them. His favorite is Sherlock Holmes, and he reads them out loud to me. He says you're a real Sherlock. Can you do card tricks like Denny?"

"Afraid not. I'm not so entertaining as he." Jasper rose and nodded at the matron. "Excuse the intrusion, ma'am."

"Of course, detective. You are a known name around here." Her smile was warm, though weary. "I'm Mrs. Yale."

Jasper patted Eddy's arm. "Will you be all right for a minute if I talk to Mrs. Yale?"

The boy nodded. "But don't leave without saying bye. I can't

By Amber Schamel

chase after you like Denny does."

Great. Hopefully, he didn't just get another tagalong. He followed Mrs. Yale into the hall.

"Would you prefer the kitchen? I can put on some tea or coffee."

"No, quite all right, I won't take much of your time. I see you're a busy woman."

A pair of children ran past them and clambered up the stairs laughing and squealing. "Jane, Lucas—" They were both gone before the words left her mouth. "Oh dear. I do apologize, detective."

"I was a child once, too." His gaze followed their direction. "Not so much unlike them."

Indeed, had it not been for Mr. and Mrs. Rudin, he may have ended up in an orphanage or home of some kind. His mother had confessed to considering it before she found work at the Rudins' mansion.

"They are sweet children, but I struggle to keep up with them these days. Ever since my dear husband passed on, I—" She inhaled a shaky breath. "Let's just say I would be lost without the kind people of the community."

Something upstairs clattered to the floor with a breaking crash. Mrs. Yale hefted her skirts to dart upstairs when a young woman jogged out of the kitchen. "I'll see to them, Mrs. Yale."

Jasper squinted. "Miss Leslie?"

She was halfway up the stairs when she glanced back. "Good evening, detective. Do excuse me."

His mouth dropped as she disappeared beyond the banister,

her heels clomping against the wooden floor.

"That girl is an angel in shoe leather." Mrs. Yale smiled at the staircase before returning her attention to Jasper. "Now, how can I help you, detective?"

"I—um—I was hoping to ask you about Mr. Gustov Rudin. I understand that you know him."

"Yes, of course. He's been such a generous patron of this home." She pointed to a corridor left of them. "That is the Rudin Wing. Completely financed by the Rudin family."

"The entire wing?" He climbed a few steps and scanned the line of doors on either side.

"Yes. A whole wing of boys' rooms. One of them is Eddy's."

Placing a hand on one of the doorknobs, he raised a brow. "May I?"

Mrs. Yale shooed him on with her hands. "By all means."

He opened the door and poked his head inside. The room held two bunk beds and a chest of drawers. "How many boys do you house in the Rudin wing?"

"There are six rooms, and we have three or four boys in most of them, so about twenty."

Jasper pulled the notepad from his pocket and jotted down the number. How could Mr. Rudin say his life had come to nothing? Jasper hadn't created a place for twenty boys to call home and be cared for. A place where dear ladies like Mrs. Yale would give them a mother's love.

Footsteps tromped down the wooden staircase. Miss Leslie descended holding a tray.

"Is everything all right?" Mrs. Yale bit her lip. "It wasn't Izzy, was it?"

"Yes and no. Izzy is fine. Lucas and Jane were trying to cheer her and upset the soup bowl. It fell off the side table. The bowl smashed to pieces, but everyone is fine."

With her sleeves rolled up and several strands of hair loose and floating beside her face, Miss Leslie could have modeled for an Edmund Blair Leighton portrait. Jasper blinked several times. Was this really the troll of the employment department?

She swept toward the kitchen but tossed a glance over her shoulder. "Her fever broke."

Mrs. Yale let out a sigh of relief. "Thank God." She turned back to Jasper. "Was there anything else, detective?"

"Hmm?" He dragged his gaze from the empty doorway Miss Leslie had passed through. "Oh, I won't keep you much longer. Tell me, where does the funding for the daily operation come from? Is Mr. Rudin responsible for that as well?"

"In part, but a lot comes from others in the community and sometimes churches."

"And your volunteers, are their services encouraged by Mr. Rudin?"

"Volunteers?"

"Yes, ma'am. Such as Miss Leslie."

Mrs. Yale's brow scrunched. "If you mean to ask whether Bet is here of her own initiative or because her employer somehow required it, I will tell you Miss Leslie has been my most loyal support for five years now. Long before she began working at Rudin Factory. She is the only one of his employees who has entered these doors. Until now, of course."

"I see." Clearing his throat, Jasper extended a hand. "I will take up no more of your time. I appreciate your cooperation. I'll just say goodbye to Eddy and be one my way."

She gave his hand a squeeze. "You're quite welcome, detective. Please let me know if I can be of help. And you are always welcome to visit. The boys would love to hear your stories."

Stories. He had none to tell. He started for the parlor, and then stopped. "Oh, Mrs. Yale, does Denny, I mean, is he—are one of those rooms his?"

She offered him a tight smile. "Not anymore. We had several younger children who needed a place, and Denny is of the age…Well, we had to find other arrangements. His home is with another family who has agreed to board him until he reaches eighteen."

That could only be a few months. "And then?"

"Then…it's in God's hands."

Chapter Eight

December 4, 1913

Jasper glared out his apartment window. A fine time for a blizzard. The wind howled as it whipped snow this way, then that, finally landing in a drift. Why did this storm seem intent on crippling all transportation in Denver?

At least the newspaper had printed a minuscule apology beside all the blizzard articles. Still, he had two cases in the balance. He needed interviews, research from the factory, records from public offices, and a meeting with his old friend from Pinkerton. The survival of the factory, and of Mr. Rudin, depended on him.

Still, it snowed. And snowed. And snowed.

Two feet of slushy white obstructed the streets. Abandoned automobiles created mounds alongside the road. Every window of the hotel down the street was illuminated. He flipped open his pocket watch. Two o'clock. Yet the gloom made it seem much

75

later.

The warmth of his apartment should have comforted him. Why then did he feel so annoyed? He poured another mug of coffee, but didn't sit. Good thing he wasn't an author. His backside was done with sitting after the last six hours. The notepad on the table held five pages of praise to Mr. Rudin and the difference his life and influence had made to those around him. The love of his wife, the existence of his daughter, the factory and the two hundred people it employed, the orphanage wing and the score of boys who had a safe living environment because of his generosity. It was all there. But he'd hoped to gain additional information from a few employees, as well as the priest.

What irked him most was not having thought to grab Mr. Stosch's file. He suspected the man had something to do with the factory mishaps, and he wanted to dig into it as soon as possible. Maybe even follow the man around a few evenings and see what he spent his time on. With such a repulsive personality, the man couldn't have friends.

Jasper snorted. As if he were any different. Where were his friends?

Knock, knock, knock.

Nonsense. Jasper shook his head. No way had he really heard a knock. It would be too on cue. Besides, no one ever visited him. Especially in a blizzard.

He lifted the mug of steaming coffee to his lips, but instead dribbled it all over his shirt. That *was* a knock on his door. Louder this time.

By Amber Schamel

He grabbed a napkin and dabbed at his shirt as he shuffled to the door. "Who's there?"

"It's me, boss. Denny."

Jasper unbolted the door and opened a crack. "Dash it, Denny, what are you doing out in a blizzard?"

The lad shrugged. "I got bored, so I came to see if you need anything."

Not sure he believed the tale, Jasper opened the door. "I suppose you might as well come in."

"Thanks." With a wide grin, Denny loped inside. "Cozy place. A little big for only one person."

Jasper glanced around the apartment. Hardly what he'd call "big" regardless of how many occupied the space. "Don't you have—" He stopped short as he remembered Mrs. Yale's remark. Denny didn't have parents, but wasn't there someone to worry about him?

"Have what?" The kid peered honestly at him with deep-brown eyes.

"Folks who will wonder where you are?"

"Nah, they don't care. Mrs. Braugh has a passel of her own kids to chase around. If I'm not taking up space, she's happier." He took off his tattered brown jacket and slung it over a chair. "So what are you working on? Any leads on the culprit?"

"I didn't learn much at the newspaper office, so I'm still mulling over the information I have."

Denny rolled his shirtsleeves up to his elbows. "What's all this?" He gestured to the pages spilling from Jasper's notebook.

"A project for Mr. Rudin." Jasper didn't care to explain it to

By Amber Schamel

the errand boy. Wasn't the kid too young for such talk anyway? Besides, he couldn't risk gossip if Denny didn't know how to keep information to himself. "I met a friend of yours yesterday."

"Of mine?"

"Eddie, a boy at the orphanage near Mr. Rudin's home."

Denny's brow dipped. "Why were you at the orphanage?"

"Just asking a few questions for this project."

"Something to do with all the money Mr. Rudin gives them?"

Jasper tilted his head. "Yes. Something to do with that. They told me you used to live at the orphanage."

With a shrug, Denny ran his hand along the back of a kitchen chair. "Yeah. Eddie's a good kid. Likes to hear all about you."

"He likes to throw snowballs better."

The dimple showed. "He gotcha, huh?"

Jasper couldn't help but return Denny's grin. "I got him, too, though."

They both laughed, but they soon fell into silence. Jasper swallowed. What thoughts pelted through Denny's mind? Were Mr. and Mrs. Braugh rough with him? "I was surprised to encounter Miss Leslie there as well."

"Of course. If Bet's not at work, she's there. Or at her sister's." He raised his gaze to meet Jasper's, and an ornery glint flashed. "You *encountered* her, huh? Sounds exciting."

Heat surged up Jasper's neck, crowned his head, and spread into his ears. "I was—uh—surprised. I didn't know she cared for charity."

A grin stretched across the boy's face, revealing his large, round eyeteeth. He pulled out a chair, settled into it, and laced his fingers across his middle. "Well, maybe you don't think she's a troll after all."

Jasper picked up the dirty dishes and carried them to the sink. "My opinion hasn't changed much."

Denny laughed. "You and Bet...you...Bet?" This time he threw his head back and howled.

Crossing his arms, Jasper glared. "Don't be ridiculous. I knew there was a reason I didn't want little boys pestering me."

"Ha, I'm a little too old to be oblivious. You're wishing I was a harmless little boy." Denny wiped tears from his eyes. "You bet."

With a growl, Jasper stalked back to the window. Would it ever stop snowing?

Denny followed him. "You know, detective, you can't fall in love and get married to Bet."

Glancing over his shoulder, Jasper arched a brow. "What's this? Does Denny the errand boy speak sense?"

"It would absolutely ruin your appeal as a Sherlock Holmes character."

Rolling his eyes, Jasper returned to his study of the large, clumpy snowflakes. "Don't start with the comparison again. I resent it."

"Have you even read it?"

Jasper jumped when Denny poked his ribs.

"Of course not. Such fancified accounts would spoil my logical processes."

"All right, let's see your logical processes at work." He

crossed his arms and puffed out his chest. "What do you know about me?"

Biting the inside of his cheek, Jasper contemplated the boy. "Mrs. Braugh doesn't feed you much. You hate being alone. You've had to fend for yourself all your life. You especially love the link sausages from Jorges's shop. I also say you play the trumpet and gamble at a pub after work."

Denny's eyes widened. "I—"

Jasper held up a finger. "I'm not quite done."

The kid clamped his mouth shut.

"The only thing frightening you more than being abandoned is me finding out what the kind folks at the orphanage know about you. And the only family you've ever known is your brother, Eddie."

Denny shoved his hands into his pockets and rocked back on his heels, refusing to meet Jasper's gaze. "Eddie isn't my brother. That's false, so how do you know anything else you've said is true?"

"Your jacket smells distinctly of Jorges's sausages, and you have a yellow mustard stain on your lapel."

"Sure, the sausages are easy enough, but you can't prove the rest."

"Every time I see you, you smell like food, and you constantly accept candies and food from everyone you come in contact with, yet you stay skinny as a tram rail. Therefore, I can only conclude that you're not fed much at home. Watching you interact with others, I can tell you've gained a talent for making friends and getting what you want because you've had to watch

By Amber Schamel

after yourself."

Denny straightened a chair with his foot. "You already knew I was an orphan, so it isn't impressive. What about the trumpet?"

"You have a musician's mark on your thumb. I know you don't play in a school band, but you must play somewhere. Your hair often smells like smoke, and I've spotted ash on your trousers. Eddie mentioned you know card tricks. Now, if I were a young man looking to make some extra money with a trumpet and cards, where would I go?"

The boy's lips pressed into a tight line, and his face colored. "I have to do something. I can't stand it at that tiny house with all those rascal kids and the way she yells all the time. And I've got to make some money, or I won't be able to live."

Jasper tipped the boy's chin, drawing Denny's brown eyes to his. "There are better ways to make money, kid."

Anger flickered in his dark eyes. He jerked from Jasper's grasp and faced the door. "Like what? You won't let me be your assistant. At this point, I'm doomed to errand boy indefinitely."

With a wince, Jasper sank onto a chair. "Mr. Rudin doesn't have a position for detective's assistant."

"He'd make one if you said you needed it."

That much might be true. Jasper rubbed his fingers together. If he let the kid share his apartment, he could probably keep the same wage as an errand boy. He only had one bedroom, but Denny could take the sofa in the main room.

He'd have to talk this over with his mirrors later.

Denny let out a long sigh. "How did you know I had a brother?"

By Amber Schamel

"Details, my boy. Details. The way Eddie talked, it seemed you two were pretty close. I figured a boy like you wouldn't take such a liking to a younger boy unless you had a connection."

Denny peered at Jasper over his shoulder. "That's it? They didn't say anything else?"

"If by 'they' you mean Eddie or Mrs. Yale, then no, not much more. Though with as sensitive to the subject as you seem to be, I feel I should go back and ask more questions."

"It's none of your business." Denny grabbed his jacket and strode toward the door.

"Detectives are nosey."

Denny spun around. "Well, you ought to keep your nose in the cases it belongs in. Where's your smart conclusions on the factory incidents?"

"I have a few. Though the case hasn't provided as many clues as you have."

"Then put your nose to work sniffing out more clues. Isn't that your job?"

Land's sake. Such a tantrum. It piqued Jasper's curiosity. But getting the kid riled up wasn't going to help anything. Especially if Denny was going to have to stay until the weather let up. Jasper wasn't sure he had the patience to have someone else around all the time. Guess this would be a good test.

Wait a minute. How did Denny get here in the first place? With all the streetcars out of commission, and the streets too obstructed for his bicycle…

"Calm down, kid. It's not as if you can just sashay out of here unless you have a pair of wings parked outside the door."

By Amber Schamel

Denny's shoulders loosened a little, and one side of his mouth tipped up. "Almost." He opened the door and grabbed a set of long thin boards curved upward at the ends.

"Skis? Can you get around with those things in this weather?"

"Well enough. They glide right over the snow, so as long as the wind isn't unbearable, I do fine."

Peering toward the window, Jasper squinted. This could be helpful.

"You want a taste of detective work, huh?" He turned back to Denny. "All right, I'll let you in on this one. But you must do exactly as I say."

Denny's eyes brightened. "You bet!" He snickered.

Jasper narrowed his brows into a glare. "Don't make me change my mind."

The kid chomped down on his lip. "Sorry."

"You can stay with me tonight. Then first thing in the morning, I'll send you on a couple of errands, and we'll see what we can find."

Rubbing his hands together, Denny grinned. "We're going to make a great team. You'll see."

Sure.

Jasper leaned back and crossed one leg over the other. "We'll start with a test. Tell me what you've gathered about the case thus far."

Folding one arm over his middle, Denny scratched his chin with his other hand. "Well, whoever it was got access to the factory's inner rooms somehow. So he or she either is a factory

By Amber Schamel

employee, buying off an employee, or gained entrance without being noticed."

"Right. They stole a key from Mr. Rudin's office. That's how they gained entrance, but still, they had to know where to find it."

"Our biggest factor would be to discover a motive, but that is so broad at this point it isn't much help. Next, we need to analyze every possible clue. We have two incidents to pull from. The first I would examine is point of entry. For the crystallization incident, the culprit used a key, but how did they get inside the building in the first place?"

Jasper's brows rose. The kid did have some deductive skill after all. "They could have slipped inside without notice somehow. Or they were already in the building."

"What about the lab? Did you figure entry there?"

"The lock wasn't picked. So either a key was used in that instance as well, or it is possible he came in through a window. One was unlocked."

Denny snapped his fingers. "After you and Charlie started on the hair mess, I checked a few windows in the Crystallization Room. One was unlocked there as well."

"Brilliant. Perhaps you do have the making of a detective. Still, if he'd used a window, why did he take the key?"

A frown puckered Denny's brow. "Good point. I wish I would have thought to check other windows. What about the window in Mr. Rudin's office? It was unlocked when I brought the message from Bet."

Pointing one of his long fingers at the boy, Jasper winked.

"There's a good eye. Wonderful observation. Did you also notice if the carpet below the window was damp?"

Denny dropped into the chair across from him. "No. I didn't get that close."

"Now, that could either mean the intruder had gone in prior to our visit, or Mr. Rudin simply opened it to look out at the weather, which is highly probable. Not knowing what time the culprit slipped in to take the key is a hindrance."

"Right. So do you have any suspects?"

"Everyone is suspect, my boy. Even Mr. Rudin himself is suspect at this point. It is vital that a detective draw no conclusions or preconceived ideas until he has enough facts to prove it. Surmising prematurely fogs the logical processes of the mind and distorts judgment and deduction."

Denny propped an elbow on the table and rested his chin on his fist. "That's exactly what Sherlock Holmes says."

"Well, in that one point, the author is correct." Jasper stood and scowled out the window once again. Dash this snow. "Denny, in your gallivanting about town, have you noticed where the Wobblies hold their meeting?"

"Out on Broadway, I think."

Brilliant. This kid might be of some use after all. Tomorrow, if this confounded snow would let up, they'd gain some momentum in solving both cases.

By Amber Schamel

Chapter Nine

December 5, 1913

Frigid snow crept in the sides of Jasper's shoes as he trudged through the street. Men and boys alike swarmed like living flurries, shoveling snow, piling it into wagons, and hauling it out of the city. Hopefully, they would get enough snow moved so the streetcars could resume operation tonight. In the meantime, Jasper would use this congregation of men in the street to gain some ground on this case.

A tall man walked alongside a horse as it towed a wagon through the drifts. Jasper fell into step beside him. "Quite the operation here."

The man shrugged. "Most snow I've ever seen, and I was spawned here."

"All these men answered the newspaper ad for employment?"

"I did. A man with a family to feed can't sit idle just because

87

it decides to blizzard. We have to get the city back to running as quickly as we can."

"I'm certainly in favor of that. My work is behind, too." Jasper paused as they passed through another deep drift. "What do the Wobblies think about this snow organization?"

"I haven't seen any of 'em around. Funny now that you mention it. Can't be long before one shows. Anywhere men are gathered, one stands up to talk."

"You're right, indeed." Jasper stepped back on the sidewalk. "Take care now."

The man nodded and continued down the road.

Jasper swiveled to take in the scene. The streets were mounded with automobiles half buried in white fluff. He chuckled and approached a Model T. Someone had built a snowman in the driver's seat. The city hadn't lost its sense of humor in the storm.

He turned down Fourteenth Avenue and headed toward the Capitol Building. If the Wobblies were going to surface anywhere, that'd be the place.

By the time he sighted the building, a young man was already standing atop a square pillar calling out to those passing by with shovels and barrels full of snow. Below him, another man stood with an armful of pamphlets. The man's posture seemed somehow familiar.

Something inside Jasper's shoe sloshed between his toes as he quickened his pace. As he neared, he ground his teeth. He'd recognize those drooping eyes anywhere. He knew the old secretary had to be one of them. But where was Mr. Stosch's

By Amber Schamel

monocle? Perhaps he didn't wear it out of doors.

Hoping to avoid notice, Jasper snatched a shovel leaning against a brick building and hefted a load of snow from the sidewalk. Working would make him less conspicuous as he listened to the Wobbly speaker.

"Look at all of us out here slaving away in the frigid weather while all the bosses sit at home before their cozy fires. We have as much in common with them as ants have with last year's derby winner. It's time we bind together and make the changes leading to a better world with equal wages for all."

Jasper stifled a guffaw. Funny that the man standing around lecturing instead of working would make such a statement. He was too boxed in to his own thinking to realize that if all had equal wages it would leave no opportunity for anyone to get ahead. It would make all equally poor, not equally rich.

The wind kicked up, and the two Wobblies braced against a gust of snow. The speaker climbed down and uttered something Jasper couldn't hear to Stosch. Then both men tramped down the street in the opposite direction.

"Hey!" A man had emerged from the alley and pointed a finger at Jasper. "Where are you taking my shovel?"

"Oh, is this yours?" He pushed it at the man. "I was just finished, anyway."

Free of the shovel, he scanned the white streets for the Wobbly men. Snow clung to everything. Even the electric wires hanging over the street were coated with ice and clumps of snow. At last, he sighted them veering into an alley.

He trotted along the sidewalk, running one hand along the

89

building to keep from falling. He peeked down the alley in time to see the two turn a corner. The crunch of their footsteps echoed off the brick walls, growing louder as he gained on them. Finally, they stopped before a storefront. A globe with the inscription Industrial Workers Of The World adorned the window.

Stosch flicked open his pocket watch. "I told you we'd be late. Walsh is going to be upset."

The one who had done the speaking pulled the door open. "Relax, Walter. These meetings never start on time."

With that, the two disappeared inside the building.

If only he could somehow get an ear in that meeting. Jasper circled around to the rear of the building. He scanned the exterior for an open window. Of course, they'd have to be crazy to have opened a window as the blizzard abated, but maybe one was broken.

He exhaled. No such luck. Although he did spot a vent along the side. Thank the Lord.

Crouching down, he listened. Faint voices, but no discernible words. He glanced around to make sure no one had spotted him, and then inched closer to the vent, straining to hear.

Mumbling. Maybe greetings. Someone clapped as if calling to order. One of them had a voice that would put anyone to sleep with its low monotonous tone.

"Did you see the article about Rudin company?" A high-pitched nasally voice was loud enough to make out. "I think we can use it to our advantage. Rudin has been the most stubborn out of all the capitalists in Denver. If he goes down, one of our largest obstacles would be out of the way."

Easy, detective. Don't draw conclusions too hastily.

More murmuring.

"Don't be worried, Mr. Stosch. If Rudin goes down, his employees will find work at one of the other factories. Hopefully, a unionized one. Then they'd be better off. We'd be doing them all a favor."

At least Stosch had voiced some concern for poor Mr. Rudin's company.

The wind whistled above Jasper's head. Snowflakes melted on his lips as he held his breath, listening. His knees cramped, but he sat for several more minutes. Finally, he gave up. Unable to make out anything more, he stood and took a few deep breaths. He needed to get out of sight before they disbursed into the street. They obviously intended to exploit Mr. Rudin and his company as much as possible. But what did that mean? What would be their next move?

He slogged from the alley and rushed toward his apartment. Denny should be waiting with Mr. Stosch's file. Jasper already gained most of the information he sought, but it wouldn't hurt to take a look. He had to figure out where these puzzle pieces fit into the picture before the Wobblies created more problems for Rudin Sugar Company.

Shopkeepers added tinsel and brightly wrapped packages to their windows as he passed. One more reminder—his time was ticking away. When at last he reached the top of the stairs, Denny was leaning the apartment door. "You look mad. What'd I miss?"

By Amber Schamel

Jasper unlocked the door and shooed the kid inside. "Do you have Stosch's file?"

"Yeah."

"Was anyone else at the factory?"

"Only Charlie. Said he'd come to check on things since he lives close by. He let me in for the file." Denny raised one brow. "You know Bet won't be happy to see a file missing, though."

"How will she know? Did you make it obvious you'd been there?"

"I left a note on her chair. 'With deepest affection, I have taken your files. With loving insults, Jasper.'"

Were all seventeen-year-olds this annoying? Jasper shrugged out of his coat and plucked the file from Denny's hand. "I've been spying on the Wobblies. Guess who I saw."

"Miss Leslie."

Jasper shot the kid a glare. One corner of Denny's mouth twitched upward. "Okay, someone not so pretty." Denny snapped his fingers. "I know, Benjamin Franklin."

"Mr. Stosch." Jasper snatched up a towel and tossed it at wide-eyed Denny. "Clean up the mess you tracked in. You know, you can stomp off most of the snow before you enter the lobby."

Denny stooped and swiped the floor, then spoke with his head down as he worked. "Where did you see him?"

"Two Wobblies were speaking near the Capitol Building. I followed them to the IWW headquarters and listened in on their meeting." Jasper dropped the file on the table and sat.

"What'd you find out?"

By Amber Schamel

"A detective doesn't often 'find out' anything. He collects facts and resists drawing conclusions from said facts until he has enough of them to piece together a logical picture." He flipped open the file. Just as he thought. "Frank Stosch, hired June 1904."

"Almost ten years of working for Mr. Rudin. Why would he try to harm the man after all that time?" Denny plunked into the chair across from Jasper and leaned over the table. "Any records of disputes? When was his last raise? Did he get passed up for a promotion?"

Indeed, the man had been secretary to Mr. Rudin since Jasper had tagged along to the factory when he was Denny's age. Of course, when he became the private investigator for the company four years ago, he had run checks on all of the current employees. They'd weeded out a few unsavory characters then. Had they missed one? Who else would have access to accomplish sabotage such as this?

*****

The next week brought sunshine and, with it, a breakthrough of gloom. Rays of rainbow light filtered through the stained-glass windows of the Holy Transfiguration Cathedral as Jasper exited the priest's office and stepped into the sanctuary. He paused before the altar. Tiny flickers danced from the multitude of candles spread about it.

Although he didn't believe God needed a candle to hear him, he took a moment to breathe a prayer of thanksgiving. The streetcars had reopened, allowing him those last few interviews he'd needed. None too soon.

By Amber Schamel

Now, under his left arm, he cradled his report on the life of Mr. Rudin, along with notes from his conversation with the priest. By the time his employer finished reading it, he'd have no doubt that his life meant something. No one could deny the pages of testimony and figures he'd rounded up.

"I see you're still a praying man, Jasper boy." Mr. Rudin's mustached tone startled him. He hadn't noticed him seated on the lone pew at the back of the room.

The bench groaned as Jasper sat beside him. "My mother did raise me before she passed. I remember quite a few conversations about the subject between the two of you."

The man grunted. "Yes, seemed to be one of her favorite topics. I never could avoid it."

"Are you not here for prayer then, Mr. Rudin?"

The old man's mouth twisted. "I'm not sure, really. I wanted to see the place since they've made improvements. And I needed a quiet place to think. This seemed a logical location."

They sat in silence, eyes wandering from stained-glass windows, to paintings and relics, finally to the imitation of Christ hanging on the Cross.

Mr. Rudin sighed and folded his arms. "I've been waiting to hear from you. Less than eighteen days left, you know."

Swallowing hard at the reminder, Jasper gripped the report. "Well, I think you will forget your countdown when you read this." He set the stack of papers between them on the bench. "I must say I am amazed. Even with as much as I knew about you and what you've meant to my family."

A strange light flickered in the man's ice-blue eyes. His

fingers fidgeted on the bench before inching toward the report. "May I?"

Jasper rose and brought a candle lamp nearer the bench. "Please do, sir."

After extracting spectacles from his pocket and adjusting them on his nose, Mr. Rudin picked up the report. His eyes slowly followed each line. Jasper paced to the front of the church and traced the embroidery of the silk linens draped across the pulpit. Somewhere beyond the iconed walls, a choir's hymn echoed, lending to the celestial aura.

"Oh, is that what they've done with that wing?" Mr. Rudin's mustache twitched as he grinned. "I'm glad the orphanage has been putting it to good use. Bunks! What a lovely idea."

Jasper held a finger to his lips. "Please, sir, the church."

Mr. Rudin shrugged, flipped the page, and rested one elbow on the back of the pew as he continued reading.

Folding his hands behind his back, Jasper returned to sit beside him. Indeed, the wing in the orphanage was a wonderful addition. Jasper's mind wandered back to Eddie and the other children. He'd have to stop by on his way home. Mr. Rudin would probably even give him a sack of candy to take to them.

Would Miss Leslie be going this afternoon? Perhaps he could catch her before she left, and they could walk there together. The thought sounded pleasant until he recalled her antagonistic nature.

Never mind.

"My wife said that?"

Jasper looked up to see Mr. Rudin's shadowed eyes pooling

with tears, searching Jasper's in the dim light as if for a life-and-death answer. "Yes, sir. It's clear she admires you very much."

Mr. Rudin reached up and dabbed the edge of his eye. "She did at one time, but I'm afraid I ruined it long ago. If you ever marry, son, don't fall off the hero's pedestal she put you on."

Frowning, Jasper cocked his head to one side. He opened his mouth to ask more, but Mr. Rudin cleared his throat and tapped the paper. "Where did you come up with these figures?"

"I—uh—calculated them myself based on the comments of those I spoke to."

An eyebrow ticked. Silent again, Mr. Rudin turned another page. He twisted his mustache. Gnawed his lower lip. Clicked his fingernails. Then chewed them. Finally, he flipped the last page and removed his spectacles.

"It is a fine report, my boy. I never knew I hailed such praise from those around me."

A grin split Jasper's face. This would do the trick.

"It would make a fine eulogy at my funeral."

The grin disappeared. "What?"

"I'd be pleased if you would read it at the service. Here, in this cathedral."

"B–but, Rudin—"

"Yes, reading this I see that ending my life before the New Year is the best plan."

"Sir!" Jasper sprang to his feet, his protest amplified by echoing room. "How can you say that? Have you not understood a word you read?"

"Calm down, Jasper. Of course, I did."

The calmness in which Mr. Rudin spoke unnerved him. The elder man rose and waved him toward the door.

"You can't take your life. Don't you see how much good you've done? How much you are revered throughout Denver?"

When they exited through the strong oak doors, Mr. Rudin faced him. "Son, there comes a point in one's life when you realize all the good you could ever do has already been done. Continuing on my current path, I will only tarnish what deeds and reputations I have previously earned."

Jasper wanted to grab the old man by the shoulders and give him a good shake. He waved his hands up toward the steeple towering over their heads. "Don't you think that should be God's call?"

Mr. Rudin followed his indication, his gaze resting on the wooden Cross above the pointed arch doorway. "Sometimes God provides the means and leaves the end to us."

"What about those around you who will suffer grief? What about your wife and daughter?"

"My daughter loves me only for the position and finances I gave her. I've made many mistakes in my life, one of them being a belief that a man could buy a child's affection. It plows a shallow ditch where only superficial love can grow. Do you know I only see my grandchild once a year? We've deliberately crossed town to visit them, but she was so busy flitting from one social gathering to another that she didn't even have time for her parents to kiss their grandson. She is content for us to send the child gifts several times a year."

"And your wife?"

Mr. Rudin's gaze faltered. He extracted gloves from his coat pocket and fit them on. "Olivia and I have seen better days. Her opinion of me is not what it used to be. My only hope is to keep it from tumbling further."

An icy breeze licked up snowflakes and flung them into Mr. Rudin's eyes. He blinked rapidly and angled toward where his chauffeur waited beside his limousine. Jasper trotted to keep up with him. "Excuse me for saying so, sir, but that is pure rubbish. I spoke personally with Mrs. Rudin—"

The man jerked around, his eyes narrowing into a sharp look that halted Jasper's words. "Do you really think my wife would reveal her personal feelings to you, Jasper boy?"

Chomping down on his lip, Jasper winced. Were things really so dire between the two of them? Perhaps that was a main reason for his employer's depressed state. There had to be a way to right it. He huffed a breath of cold air. "She did mention you haven't been yourself. She's concerned for you, sir."

The door clicked as the chauffeur swung it open. Mr. Rudin braced one hand on the top, ready to duck inside. "Concern is an easy emotion, dear boy. If you'd lived with anyone forty years, you'd be inhuman not to have a 'concern' for them." He paused as a streetcar rumbled passed with a trill of the trolley bell. "Everyone would be better off with the money and memories I would leave behind. Memories grow fonder after one has passed, you know."

"Mr. Rudin, that simply isn't true."

The man lowered into his seat in the car, icy-blue eyes penetrating as his hand lingered on the door. "Then prove it,

98

detective."

By Amber Schamel

Chapter Ten

Brilliant. Now what?

Jasper's teeth clenched as he strode down Lincoln Street. He'd spent hours—days, actually—compiling that report. He was so sure it would be what he needed to convince Mr. Rudin. Instead, it had done the opposite.

There was no humanly possible way to change a stubborn man's mind. And he was running out of time.

He passed a group of carolers perched on the side of the road singing "Joy To The World". Why couldn't Mr. Rudin pick up on a little of that "joy of the season"?

Frigid air caught the edges of Jasper's coat, lifting it out of the way, and encircled his waist, providing a welcome contrast to the blood boiling in his veins. Balling his fists, he lengthened his strides. The man was insufferable. And his ridiculous notions. He was as emotional as a schoolgirl.

Jasper turned a corner. But his shoe slipped on the icy walk, and he collided with a young woman. She let out a shriek before sprawling into the slush pile edging the street. He landed with a slosh in a mud puddle beside the stack of books she'd been toting.

"Oh." The lady's hat had fallen over her eyes, and she flung her hands to rid her gloves of snow and filth. "Why don't men ever watch where they're plowing their brute forms? Just look at this mess." She pushed her hat up, and he recognized her hazel eyes as she gazed at the stack beside him. "And just look at those books. They were supposed to be a Christmas gift for the children at the orphanage."

Her eyes met his, and her lips puckered. "You! I might have known."

"Me? And what about you, Miss Leslie? Shouldn't you have watched where you were going, too? I hardly think you can say I'm the only one at fault. I'm more soiled than you are."

"You were soiled to begin with. Now your suit matches your sour face and mood."

"My face? My mood?" Jasper pressed himself off the pavement and shook his leg, water spewing as he did. "If I weren't a gentleman—"

"A gentleman? No, sir. A gentleman would apologize and help a lady retrieve her belongings. Perhaps even offer to pay for what he damaged."

If it weren't for his mother's voice echoing in his memory, he'd have left the woman in the snow pile and continued on his way. Instead, he offered his hand. She took it, though scowling as she did, and he lifted her out of the snow. Her gloved hand felt so tiny inside his. A strange numbness tingled up his forearm.

Once she was steady, he bent and picked up the books. Wiping mud from the covers with his scarf, he read the titles— Adventures Of Sherlock Holmes and The Works Of Shakespeare.

"You don't have very good taste in literature, Miss Leslie. Novels and love operas are hardly fitting. You might find something more substantial to feed young minds."

She snatched the books away from him, wisps of damp hair clung to both of her flaming cheeks. "Not that they'll even get to read them now."

"Don't be silly. The covers are a little moist, but the books will be fine once they dry out."

"Fine." She folded her arms across the books and eyed him. The same angry green predominant in her gaze. "Well? Are you going to apologize?"

Jasper snorted. "I might." He brushed past her. "If I'd run into a lady."

He didn't look back as he crossed the street and continued down the other side. But he could hear her huff before her quick steps charged in the opposite direction. It was almost worth the chiding voice of his mother echoing in his head all the way home. Really, he'd controlled himself pretty well considering his fury. Consoling himself with this thought, he unlocked his apartment door and entered the cramped space.

He hung his wet coat and plucked off his shoes. Socks, however, didn't come so easily. He nearly toppled three times

By Amber Schamel

before he peeled them off. Cold. Wet. And all the fault of that troll of a woman. Of course, that wasn't even the worst of it. He snatched the cover from his bed, wrapped it around his shoulders, and stalked to the sitting area. He scowled before the golden mirror.

"You lied. You told me it would work." His eyebrows dipped further as he stared at his reflection. "You needed it. A little humility can be a good thing."

He pulled the blanket tighter and sniffed. "Not that pride has ever been one of my faults."

Laughter came from somewhere. Out the window? Jasper shook his head.

Focus, detective.

"So, what are we supposed to try next?" He blinked several times, but the gold mirror gave him no answers. He faced the dark one. "Well?"

Still nothing.

Turning again, he faced the plain mirror this time and rubbed his fingers together. "The notebook."

He strode to the table and flipped it open to his original notes. PURPOSE scrawled across the top in big bold letters.

"Purpose, yes. But it needs to go a bit further this time."

He plucked up a pencil and flipped the page.

VISION.

Yes, if he could cast a vision for Mr. Rudin, show him what good he could accomplish in the coming years. Give him something to aim for, something to angle toward down the road, that would give him a reason to live.

By Amber Schamel

His mind's wheels spinning now, he pulled out a chair, tossed the blanket aside and sat before his notebook.

THINGS MR. RUDIN COULD DO/CHANGE.

He tapped his chin. The orphanage was in pretty good shape, but what if Mr. Rudin put together a program to give the boys something to do when they reached Denny's age? He could start an occupational program and help them find jobs in the community paying enough to support themselves.

Chewing the inside of his cheek, he jotted the idea down.

WIN BACK HIS DAUGHTER AND GRANDCHILD.

Although how Mr. Rudin would accomplish such a feat was yet to be known.

TAKE MRS. RUDIN ON A LAVISH TRIP. RENEW THE ROMANCE.

Jasper knew nothing of such things, but surely, it would be as easy as a trip and occasional chocolates and flowers. Except with Miss Leslie. That woman probably hated flowers and was allergic to chocolate. Trolls didn't like chocolate, did they?

What else was important to Mr. Rudin? He might expand his business and open a second factory. Perhaps he could fund some grand building and put his name to it. An everlasting memorial. One eyebrow quirked, but Jasper wrote those down anyway.

He stood, straightened his vest, and grasped his coffee cup. "Speaking of the troll." Mr. Stosch's file still sat on the table. He'd have to take it back in the morning and hope the woman had been too busy to miss it.

*****

The worst thing about snow was the mess it made when

melting. Jasper sidestepped a muddy puddle as he exited his apartment lobby. He eyed his cap-toe boots with a grunt. He'd need a new pair by the time winter was over. One more thing ruined.

"Boss, we need to get a handle on this newspaper thing. Just look." How did this kid always appear out of nowhere? Denny shoved a newspaper at Jasper's nose.

Clamping Stosch's file under his arm, Jasper swatted the paper back. "Come, Denny, I can't read anything so close. What are you blabbering on about?"

The boy thrust a finger at one of the articles.

SABOTAGE AT RUDIN FACTORY!

McCracken no doubt. Jasper thrust the paper back at Denny. "Read aloud as we walk."

The kid fell into step beside him with the newspaper folded to the article. "'Anonymous informants have advised the press of a suspected sabotage at the Rudin Sugar Factory earlier this week. The source claims human hair was planted in one of the crystallizing machines. Although the extent of the contamination is unclear, it is certain that foul play is involved. Personnel remained at the factory until late into the night salvaging the damage. Rudin Company declined to comment, but they have assigned a detective to the case.'"

"The nerve. Lord, help me. I might jar McCracken's marbles so hard he can never gather them again."

Denny nudged him with an elbow. "Easy now, he hasn't done anything illegal. It's all fact."

"Legal, maybe, but certainly unethical. And after I

specifically told him not to—" Wait. How did McCracken know which machine had been affected? He must have heard from that post boy again. Jasper's nails dug into his palms. "I told him to call me."

Jasper threw open the newspaper office door. The bang against the side of the building made the girl behind the desk jump. She whirled around from hanging tinsel, and her face went pale. "I tried to tell him, detective."

"New correspondence from your anonymous informant, I assume. When?"

She lifted a trembling hand to push a strand of stringy hair behind her ear. "Two days ago. McCracken took the boy into his office and spoke to him behind the closed door."

Jasper handed Denny the file from under his arm, pivoted, and charged for the reporter's office. The door opened, and McCracken leaned against the doorjamb. "Ah, I've been expecting you."

The challenging smirk was too much. Jasper shoved him back into the office, hardly giving Denny enough time to slip in behind him before he slammed the door. "You rat, I told you to contact me if you heard anything more, not publish it on the front page."

"You can't blame me if the leads come to me instead of you."

Gripping McCracken's shoulder, Jasper pinched. The man let out a yelp and dropped into the chair Jasper occupied during his last visit. He must have brought it in for that post boy. "No games, McCracken. What did the boy say? Who was he?"

By Amber Schamel

"Kid was paid off by some fellow downtown. He was next to useless besides the note he carried with the few specifics you hadn't provided."

He released his grip on the man's shoulder. "Where is the note?"

The paper McCracken pulled from his pocket was as rumpled as his shirt. At least he'd kept it handy this time instead of losing it in his wreckage of a desk.

Jasper studied the note. He'd printed it almost word for word in the paper. The handwriting was unfamiliar, but he could analyze it, compare it with employee signatures.

"Did you get any information on the boy? Name? Address? Where he was commissioned to deliver this?"

"He wouldn't tell me anything."

"Precisely why you should have called me. Details, people. Details." He got tired of saying that. When would people learn?

McCracken's round cheeks flushed. "You think you could have done better?"

Oh please. He didn't have time for this.

"Detectives have a little more authority to draw from, that's all." Denny smiled at the reporter. "I'm sure you did a fine job with the boy and everything you could to get answers."

Jasper cast a scowl over his shoulder. Which side was his protégé on anyway?

Denny shoved his hands in his pockets and rocked back on his heels. "The man might have told him to say nothing else to you, but the presence of an official might have scared it out of him."

McCracken's thick shoulders shrugged. "Maybe. But I doubt it."

"What else?" Jasper couldn't help the snap in his tone. The man was plain daft to let the boy slip through his fingers.

The reporter folded his arms. "Have more than you show, and speak less than you know."

Closing his eyes, Jasper counted to ten. But he was still ready to level the man when he opened them again. His hand fisted, ready to punch the lip that poked out like a defiant child's.

"You're an admirer of Shakespeare, Mr. McCracken?" Denny's dimple deepened. "Then consider, too, 'Time shall unfold what plighted cunning hides; who cover faults, at last shame them derides.' Hide your information from us, and my mentor here is sure to suspect you played a part in this crime. Or you could join forces with us. You're a smart man. But three smart men are better than one. Wouldn't it be nice to publish an article in which the detective of Rudin Sugar Company gave special mention and thanks to Mr. McCracken for his brilliant actions and assistance in solving the case?"

Brilliant was one word that should never have been used together with this man's name, but McCracken's next words kept Jasper from saying so.

"I followed the kid when he left. Seems he's a regular delivery boy at Lowell Pharmacy on Seventeenth Street."

"What did he look like?" Denny's head cocked to one side.

"Short. Brown hair. Tiny nose with a slight upturn."

With a snap of his fingers, Denny pointed. "I know the very

one. Thank you, you've been most helpful." Denny caught Jasper's arm and tugged him toward the door. "We'll have to chat with the boy right away. Have a wonderful day, sir."

Jasper planted his feet. He wasn't about to let Denny drag him out. He opened his mouth to scold the boy, but then Denny gave him a wink. "You're absolutely right, detective. It's exactly as you thought all along. This is going to be the case of the century."

What was the kid talking about? Jasper's frown deepened, but he held his tongue this time.

"Wait just a moment." McCracken shot out of the chair. "What had he thought? What makes it the case of the century?"

Denny flicked his hand. "Why should we bother to tell you when you don't even keep in touch? We do like to have reporters on our side, but we'll have to find one who's more cooperative. Lead the way, Detective Hollock."

The expression contorting McCracken's face brought a smirk to Jasper's. He couldn't help it. Chomping down hard on his lip to keep from spoiling Denny's effect, he headed toward the door with Denny right behind him.

As soon as the door clicked shut, Jasper could bear it no longer. A chuckle slipped out. "What was that all about?"

"'The robbed that smiles steals something from the thief.'" Denny's British accent was pathetic. "Another Shakespeare line."

Jasper tugged back Stosch's file. He still needed to return it. "Is it Miss Leslie filling your head with such nonsense?"

Denny laughed outright. "You bet."

By Amber Schamel

Jasper gave him an elbow in the ribs.

When they were out of sight of the door, Denny grabbed his arm and edged him into the alley, pressing a finger to his lips. He hunkered down, motioned for Jasper to follow, and crept along the side of the wall until they crouched beneath a window. As they stilled, muffled voices became audible from the other side.

"They clearly know more than they're telling me, but they won't say a word." McCracken's huffy tone. "Onerous detectives. This is why I hate their sort."

"If you'd listened to me and called them, they might give you first claim to the story. Now they'll give it to someone else just to spite you."

Either a bear from the circus had found its way into the office, or McCracken had a terrible growl.

"Oh, I'll keep in touch. I'll fill his line with calls, stalk him if I need to. Besides, I didn't spill all my information, either. They'll be back to speak to me."

By Amber Schamel

By Amber Schamel

Chapter Eleven

Jasper hated waiting, even for an important appointment. He glanced up at the clock ticking above a Christmas tree glistening beneath the silver tinsel thrown over it. The decoration seemed out of place in the bare waiting room of the Pinkerton Agency. Thirty minutes and this hard-backed chair was getting uncomfortable. At least he'd anticipated the wait and brought something productive to do. He thumbed through the dashed file he still needed to return to Miss Leslie's office. He'd been procrastinating, part of him hoping he'd find another clue if he went through it enough times. With only ten days left, he'd hardly slept this week.

"The director will see you now, Hollock." The Pinkerton secretary waved Jasper toward James's office.

"Thank you." The secretary nodded before the door shut. Jasper faced the large desk, not too different from Mr. Rudin's. Cigar smoke was thick in the little room, causing Jasper's throat

113

to tighten. Had James really painted the walls that drab brownish color? Or was it a result of the smoke?

"Well, hello, Hollock. It's been an age."

James McParland had less hair than Jasper remembered— probably due to the stress his job entailed. Being the director of the Pinkerton Detective office in Denver couldn't be an easy task. Shadowed eyes peered from behind wire spectacles that curled over ears seemingly too small for his head, and he sported the same old mustache, also similar to Mr. Rudin's.

"It has. How are you, James?"

"As well as can be expected, I suppose. Have a seat." He thrust a thick finger at the single chair upholstered with the same horrid brown color. "How are you faring at Rudin Company?"

"Well." The chair creaked as Jasper eased into it. He sat forward, hoping it wouldn't cave in on him. "Until recently. I've come upon a problem I'm having difficulty with, and I thought you might be able to help."

"With your knack, I'm surprised you need it." James's eyes twinkled, as if he remembered their first meeting more than five years ago when Jasper interned with the police department. "What can I do for you?"

"Had any run-ins with the Wobblies lately?"

With his thumb and index finger, James stroked his graying mustache. "Not anything worth noting. They persist in their same old schemes, but nothing violent. I take it you suspect them of the tampering going on at your factory?"

He must have seen the paper. Jasper twisted a button on his vest. "Whoever it is covered their tracks pretty well. I have some

By Amber Schamel

random facts, but piecing them together hasn't brought any conclusions yet. I'm missing a vital piece, and I'm not even sure what that piece is."

"Remember, every observation may be important. Don't overlook anything."

"Details…I know. How could I forget your proverb? You might as well draw it up to be your epitaph."

James chuckled. "Let's hope I don't need one too soon."

"Have you been acquainted with a reporter by the name of McCracken?"

Back to the mustache rubbing. "McCracken. Sure sounds familiar. Oh yes. The chubby fellow who likes to get in everyone's business. He's got a bit of a nose, though. Not anything like yours, but a talent. Thought about offering to train him."

"How much meddling can someone like that get away with before I can ask the authorities to intervene?"

The director chuckled and straightened a stack of paper on his desk. "Bothering you that much, is he?"

Jasper tugged his vest and cleared his throat. How did the fellow breathe in this room? "He has denied my request to contact me when he receives more information and instead takes it straight to print without verifying any facts."

"Sounds like a reporter all right. I suppose you can bluff him pretty far, but you'd have to have some proof to get him behind bars. Has he published anything faulty?"

"Not quite…though very close."

"You're stuck, then." James opened a desk drawer and

pulled out a cigar box. "Smoke?"

"No, thank you."

With a shrug, he replaced the box. "Now about these Wobblies. They've gained a lot of ground in the past year. Winning the free speech fights has emboldened them. Annoying as they are, they seem to be gaining members."

A fact Jasper well knew. Though he didn't understand it. He squeezed the bridge of his nose. "Do you think they're capable of sabotaging the companies that aren't giving in to their union rules?"

"Of course. What clues do you have that point to them?"

"Motivation, first off. I don't know of anyone else who would intend to harm Mr. Rudin and his business, but he's a fierce opponent of the IWW doctrine. The incidents have to be an employee, which I imagine is a member, or close to one. Mr. Rudin's secretary, Mr. Stosch, is linked with them."

James shrugged. "Sounds like you've got a decent sniff on it then. All you have to do is link the crimes to the secretary. Or catch him in the act. That'd be better." His gaze studied Jasper. "Why are you unsure of your conclusion?"

"I've found nothing at the scene to point to Stosch except his links to the Wobblies." Jasper held up the file with Stosch's name.

"Does it point to someone else?"

Jasper squeezed his eyes shut, replaying as many of the pictures as he could. "I don't know. Yet."

"It sounds as though you're on the right track. I'm sorry I can't be of more help. Want me to send someone to scare

McCracken?"

"Don't tempt me." Jasper stood and extended a hand. "Thanks for your time. It's good to see you."

"Likewise. Stop in again. I like to see how you're getting along. I'll follow your case in the papers."

Jasper offered a sarcastic salute and let himself out. He wasn't sure if his time for the meeting was well spent, but spent it was. Hopefully, Denny's errand was more productive. If he'd found the kid McCracken received messages from, perhaps he gained a clue or two.

He caught a trolley and hopped off in front of the factory. His long strides carried him to the employment department. Miss Leslie was not to be seen, so he slipped around her desk, hoping to return the folder before she returned. He opened the file drawer and dropped it inside, closing the drawer with a quiet thud.

When he turned, he scowled at her desk. The scent of peppermint wafted from the bulky candy canes weighting down her stack of typing paper. Everything was neat and tidy, except for several scraps of paper propped up against the wall on the right side. Manger scene drawings from children, he supposed. But which ones? Mrs. Yale and Denny had mentioned nieces and nephews. Or the orphans. Strange. Keeping children's scribble seemed too sentimental for the office troll Miss Leslie appeared to be.

Tearing his gaze away, he headed toward the main entrance. He'd wait for Denny there.

"Boss, there you are." Denny huffed as he sprinted up to

him. "Mr. Rudin's in a tizzy. A machine has broken down, and he's sure it's going to take weeks to get it fixed. You've got to help him calm down."

How could things always go from bad to worse to much worse? His boots thundered against the wood as Jasper hurried after Denny. "What about your errand. Did you find the boy?"

"Yes, but the man he described didn't sound familiar."

He'd have to get the rest of the facts later. For now, he had to deal with Mr. Rudin.

"What do you mean you can't fix it? Do you know what this will do to our production?" Mr. Rudin's raised voice met him down the hall.

"I'm sorry, Mr. Rudin, I will do the best I can." Poor Charlie wrung his hands. "We have to find the part, and I can't control how long that takes."

"Stosch, get the machine manufacturer on the telephone for me now." Mr. Rudin stormed back toward his office, leaving Charlie holding a wrench.

Jasper raised a brow. "Bad as all that?"

Charlie shrugged. "This one and the one on the end seem to have come loose of a couple bolts. Without them, the machine won't operate at all. Having two of the four not working will cut our production until I can get it fixed."

These giant machines always intimidated Jasper. But he stepped closer and peered at the large bowl and paddle held in place by three nuts and bolts. Strange. None of the other nuts on the machine seemed loose. "Go ahead and tighten the rest of the bolts to make sure none of them come off, too."

By Amber Schamel

"Sure will, detective." Charlie put the wrench he was holding to use.

Hmm. Jasper circled the machine. "How did they discover the problem?"

"There was an obstruction just before everyone left for the evening. They called me in to fix it. When I tried to restart the machine, it wasn't right. I shut it off quick as I could until I found the bolt missing. Naturally, I told Mr. Rudin right away."

"Where was the obstruction?" Jasper bent to search beneath the machine.

Charlie motioned to the tub of the boiler machine. "The bowl got gummed up and stopped the paddle."

"I see." Jasper scanned the remainder of the room but gathered no more clues. He'd best get to Mr. Rudin. "Have a good evening, Charlie."

The janitor saluted with the wrench as Jasper strode toward his employer's office, with Denny at his heels.

"Do you think the breakdown is related to the case? Seems awful strange, being so sudden."

"A wonderful observation, young Denny. Keep your eyes and ears open, and you'll learn a lot."

Mr. Rudin's voice came through the closed door when they reached his office. "Can't you get it here any faster? Do you know what a couple little nuts will do to my business?" A long pause. "That's better. Thank you.… Yes, I appreciate it.… Very good. Thanks again." The receiver clicked into place. "That's how it's done, Mr. Stosch. They'll have the missing parts here by the end of the week. Now let's figure out how we're going to

119

By Amber Schamel

keep up production with half of our machines down in the meantime. Ask Miss Leslie to meet me, please."

Stosch soon opened the door. He rolled his eyes at Jasper. "Doubt you'll be of much help in this situation."

"Hollock, get in here." Mr. Rudin's voice boomed from inside.

Jasper cringed at the rough tone. While he was growing up, Jasper could only remember Mr. Rudin being upset a few times. Less than that the times the man had raised his voice.

"I'll fetch Miss Leslie for you, Mr. Stosch." Denny pivoted on his heel and headed down the hall.

With a clearing of his throat, Jasper stepped inside and closed the door.

Mr. Rudin paced in front of the large window, his hands clasped behind his back. "This is horrible. Just horrible. All the bad publicity already, now a decrease in production and getting so close to Christmas when every sweet imaginable is in demand."

"The part will soon be replaced, and we'll carry on as usual."

"And what will be next, detective? Do you have a handle on this case or not?"

Jasper sighed. "I'm getting closer."

"Closer? Closer as in we're closer to England than India?"

With a tug at his vest, Jasper straightened. Sharp words did not come from the Mr. Rudin he knew. "Mr. Rudin, I assure you, I am working as hard as I can. We'll have this resolved soon. And I'll do whatever I can to help you through this issue." He ventured a step forward and reached out to touch his shoulder. "Uncle Rudi, it's all going to be okay, isn't it?"

Rudin's blue eyes softened at the pet name. "Oh, Jasper boy." His shoulders slouched, and he shuffled to his chair, heaving his tired form into the seat. "You haven't called me Uncle Rudi since you were a boy of ten in a baseball cap."

Jasper forced a smile. He remembered. Though he had outgrown the term, considering it technically untrue, he hadn't outgrown their bond. His heart pinched as the bags under Mr. Rudin's eyes bespoke what was at stake. And the lines in the elder man's forehead were deeper than Jasper recalled. He swallowed the emotion building in his throat. "I have made some progress on your other case, sir."

Instead of replying, Mr. Rudin buried his face in his hands and rubbed up and down.

Taking advantage of the moment, Jasper pulled out his notebook. "I believe you have lost sight of what potential your life yet has, Uncle Rudi."

Mr. Rudin's eyes peered between his fingers.

"Think of all the good you could do with your influence and experience, sir. You have done so much for those boys at the orphanage, but there's so much more you could do. You could begin a program to train them in a skill and then find them employment with other businessmen in Denver so they can support themselves and become useful members of society."

Rudin's hands dropped from his face. "A program?"

"It would be such a wonderful thing for them. Put their feet on the right path."

Tearing the list of ideas from his notebook, Jasper slid it

By Amber Schamel

across the desk. "We all have regrets, sir, but you could use these next years to reclaim what has slipped away from you. Take Mrs. Rudin on a long honeymoon, reconnect with your daughter."

Jasper held his breath as Mr. Rudin looked over his list. He opened one of his desk drawers and withdrew a pen, and then marked a star next to several items and *X*s next to others. Then he slid the paper back. Jasper frowned down at it.

"The stars are items I would like you to attend to after I'm gone. I like your program idea—you are the perfect man to see to it."

After he was gone? "But, sir—"

"The *X*s are the items that are impossible. I cannot reconnect with my daughter. She has shut me out, and I cannot blame her. I'm too late, Jasper boy. As for Mrs. Rudin, sins of my past have soiled her opinion of me, and I cannot change those. She will never forgive me, nor should she. I used her for my own selfish gain. These are things that can't be undone, and the more I have tried to correct it, the worse I make it."

Jasper opened his mouth to argue, but a knock on the door interrupted him. Miss Leslie peered in, her hazel eyes settled on Jasper. "Excuse me, Mr. Rudin. Denny said you wanted to see me, but I can come back later if you're busy."

"Come in, dear girl." Mr. Rudin's usual smile reappeared, masking the sincere desperation from a moment before. "I was hoping you could help me solve a problem."

Miss Leslie slipped inside, notepad tucked under her arm. Her head tilted in question, bringing the pencil holding her bun in place into focus. Today, her copper-brown vest and skirt somehow made her eyes seem even more prominent. "I'll be happy to, sir. What seems to be the matter?"

Mr. Rudin, surely, was hoping Jasper would take his leave and let the subject drop. Not a chance. He would stay, even if the troll did look at him as if he were a rat in a meal barrel. He planted himself in a chair and rested one leg across his knee.

"Have a seat, Miss Leslie." Mr. Rudin motioned to the chair next to Jasper.

Her long skirt brushed his shoe as she stepped over and sat. He shifted away from her and folded his arms across his chest. He could feel the throbbing of his pulse in his wrist. Funny how her entrance always seemed to be simultaneous with his temper. No matter. This interruption would soon pass, and he could resume his conversation.

Mr. Rudin rested his hands on the desk. "Two of the four boiling machines are down, and we won't be able to get them fixed until the end of the week. Obviously, this is going to be a problem with production."

Miss Leslie plucked a second pencil from her vest pocket and rolled it between her fingers. This woman must have a fetish with the things. Although, that was something Jasper could understand.

Her breath hitched before she spoke. "Perhaps we could split the shift and have the second half work through the night to keep up."

Jasper blinked. The troll did have a brain behind those sculpted brows.

By Amber Schamel

"Do you think they'd be willing to do so? I hate to interrupt their schedule, but I really see no other way."

"You're so kind, Mr. Rudin. I will speak with them, but I think I can safely say they will be glad to work through the night rather than be sent home for a week."

Mr. Rudin let out a breath, and his mouth turned upward. "Thank you, Miss Leslie. I appreciate your help. Do let me know what the boys decide."

She stood and offered him a smile as sweet as the candy on Mr. Rudin's desk. Since when had she been capable of that? "Of course, sir. Don't worry about a thing. We'll keep up." She cast a sideways glance at Jasper. "I'll not interrupt your meeting any longer. Excuse me."

She slipped out of the room as quietly as she came. Jasper leaned forward, clasping his hands. He waited for Mr. Rudin to meet his gaze, and then pushed the list back at him.

"Think about this list. Take it home. Pray over it. I'll be back tomorrow, and we can talk more."

Mr. Rudin nodded. "All right, Jasper boy. Though I warn you, I haven't been in the habit of prayer."

"I'd venture to say that's your first problem, sir."

A tilt of his head granted that, but Mr. Rudin said nothing. For now, Jasper would take what he could get. He exited Mr. Rudin's office and eyed Stosch's vacant desk. The man had been gone the last few times Jasper had come around. He couldn't really complain, but it did seem odd. Where could he possibly have an excuse to slip away to so often?

Turning down the hall, he sought Denny. He still needed to

report on his conversation with the boy from the pharmacy.

When Jasper exited the factory building, Denny was waiting beside his bicycle. "How'd it go?"

"I think he's stable. For now. Tell me about your afternoon."

Denny walked his bike along, keeping pace with Jasper as they headed down Lincoln Street toward his apartment. "I found the kid, but he was pretty tightlipped. Took me a while to coax anything out of him. He told me a man met him out on the street and paid him to deliver the note to the newspaper office."

"Did he identify who the man was?"

"He said he didn't know who he was, though he'd seen him before. Said he was of average height, dark hair, businessman by the looks of him. That's all."

Could have been Mr. Stosch. Could have been anyone. "Not terribly helpful. No identifying marks or scents?"

Denny's brows pulled together. "Scents?"

"What'd the guy smell like?"

"I didn't think to ask the kid."

Hmmph. This boy had a lot to learn. "Smells can give a lot of clues. You'll learn to pay attention to them. Ever notice how almost everyone at the factory has a hint of sweet smell?"

"I…uh…guess so."

"A mechanic smells of oil. Businessmen smell of cologne or ink or something of similar nature."

"What do I smell like?"

"Usually those sausages you like so well. Today you smell like sweat and melting snow."

Denny's eyes widened, and he sniffed his jacket self-

By Amber Schamel

consciously.

Jasper couldn't hold back a chuckle. He spun the boy's cap around. "Go home and take a bath. Bring me a newspaper first thing in the morning. We need to keep a close eye on McCracken."

"What are you going to do?"

"I'm going for a stroll. Then I'll do exactly as I've instructed you." He hoped his answer would suffice. He didn't want a kid along on his next errand.

Chapter Twelve

Jasper dragged his eyelids open and fumbled for the alarm clock clanging on the table beside his bed. He rubbed his eyes. He'd need three cups of coffee this morning.

After following the pharmacy boy around and scouting out the other end of town half the night, he was beat. And to say his feet ached would be an understatement. He cringed at the thought of wiggling into his cap-toe boots.

He put on the coffee, splashed water on his face, and changed his rumpled clothes. He inhaled deeply. *Thank You, Lord, for whoever invented coffee. It must be Your mercy on Your weary servants.* He poured a cup of the steaming liquid into his favorite mug and savored a blessed first sip.

A horn blared outside, interrupting his serene moment. He drew back the curtain and peered down at Mr. Rudin's Model 6 Berline Limousine parked at the curb. The chauffeur opened the door, stood, and waved his arms in frantic motions. What in the world?

Jasper unlatched the window and pushed it open. "What's that?"

"Hollock, get down here! Not a moment to waste."

Those words were stronger than the coffee he left on the table as he tugged the window closed. Tucking his pistol into his waistband, he dashed out the door and tore down the stairs. He slipped into the passenger side of the car, and the chauffeur slammed it into gear and tore down the street. "What's going on, Mitch?"

"The Wobblies showed up. A horde o' them."

Jasper's fists balled until his knuckles whitened. "What do they want?"

"One of the men on shift must have been upset about the schedule change and gone to them. That, combined with the logs released in the paper this morning, have them in an outrage."

"Outrage?"

"The tensions were high when Mr. Rudin sent me to fetch you. They're chanting and demanding Mr. Rudin come out to address them. He wants to, but Mr. Stosch convinced him to wait for you or the police."

"Mr. Stosch?"

Mitch glanced at him. "That surprise you?"

Avoiding the question, Jasper bit his cheek. "What did you say about the newspaper?"

"Logs bearing the Rudin Factory emblem were published containing records of a recent hair contamination and previous incidents."

By Amber Schamel

Dash it. What had McCracken gotten his hands on this time? Jasper's fingers worked his vest buttons as he thought.

"The lab." It had to be.

They curved a corner, and the factory loomed ahead. But no steam rose from the stacks. A large crowd clogged the parking lot. As the limousine swerved to the back entrance, workers stared down from factory windows.

Before Mitch could shift to park, Jasper leapt from the car and bounded inside.

Mr. Rudin met him halfway down the hall. "They're insane, Jasper boy. Insane. What should we do?"

Jasper felt for his gun. He pressed forward to the window where Mr. Stosch, Miss Leslie, and a few others were gathered.

The crowd's unified voice sent out an eerie warble. "Tyrant, tyrant, Rudin rages. No more, no more, come and face us."

The windowpane rattled beneath Jasper's fingertips.

Miss Leslie's eyes, wide and tinged with golden fear, met his. "This is my fault, detective. I asked the men to work an overnight shift to make up for the broken machines."

Jasper gave a slight shake of his head, his anger swelling. "A perfectly reasonable request, Miss Leslie." Did these Wobblies know they were intimidating a woman? A troll—though she may be—still didn't deserve to be scared out of her tiny, heeled boots by a mob. "Let me handle this, Mr. Rudin."

He started for the door, but his employer snagged his arm. "No, let me. I'm not afraid to face them. The worst they can do won't bother me."

Now who was insane? They'd likely stone him if he stepped

outside. Jasper was not about to let that happen. "That's precisely why you're staying right here." With a firm grip on the man's arm, he shoved him back a step. "I don't even want you in view of the window."

"But, Jasper, they might hurt you."

"I'll be fine, but I won't let them treat you like this, Uncle Rudi."

A click and the roar of the crowd increased. Jasper whirled around in time to see Miss Leslie slip out the door. "Bet, no!"

The door shut. He lunged for the handle and jerked it open. She stood facing the crowd, holding up one of her small hands to quiet the mob. He eased close and leaned down. "Are you out of your mind?" His whisper came out more of a hiss, which didn't help.

Her jaw tightened. "Gentlemen, please." Her delicate voice was nothing against the crowd. "This is all a misunderstanding."

"What's to misunderstand about the tyrant forcing men to work all through the night?" A man with his hands wrapped in rags strode forth.

"No, it's not that at all. We—*I*—asked the men if they'd be willing to split the shift and only for a week to compensate for a downed machine." From the front, Miss Leslie looked completely calm. But her hands wrung like a laundry machine behind her back.

"That's how it always starts. The promise of temporary until his greedy tongue gets a taste of the money. Rudin has no compassion for his workers. We'll see if his blood runs red or green."

By Amber Schamel

Miss Leslie took a step back as the crowd roared their agreement. "Gentlemen, please, be reasonable." She raised her voice, but their clamor thundered louder.

"What reason is there in letting our children be slaves in sugar factories with tyrants like him? Let the coward come out, or we'll bust his windows." The man gripped a rock and tossed it in the air, a gleam of hatred in his eye.

Jasper stepped forward, a protective grasp on Bet's elbow. "Now listen here. What good will violence do you? Do one lick of harm to this building or anyone inside, and your children will see you sent to jail and your name villainized in the papers. You fought for your right to free speech, and the same freedom applies to Mr. Rudin. He has a right to the pursuit of happiness the same as you. You can't hate a man simply because he succeeds better than you."

"An empire built on the backs of helpless workers like us!" The man raised his rag-tied hand in a fist, and his eyes flashed. "But we'll no longer allow him to force us into working all night long to produce poisoned sugar. He's an evil Russian trying to kill off the American working class. We won't stand for it!"

"The police will be here any moment. Fight with brains not stones."

"What? The brains you capitalists think we don't have?"

"You're crazy. Stand down, or I'll haul you in." Jasper advanced, reaching out to grab the man's arm, but he jerked free. "Don't let 'em, boys! Don't let them take our own."

The horde shouted and lurched as one. A stone zinged past him. Miss Leslie let out a cry. Jasper whirled as she fell to the

131

By Amber Schamel

ground, blood streaming from her temple. "Bet!"

"There he is. There's the Russian tyrant." The hothead pointed to the window. "Take him, boys!"

Before Jasper could reach Bet, the mob surged forward, pushing him farther from her. They slammed him against the brick wall. Rocks pelted the windows. Fists hammered the door at the same speed of his heart. Jasper struggled to get his hands free of the crush. If he could just reach his waistband. Finally, he gripped the pistol.

Bang.

Screams followed his gunshot, and the crowd retreated. Panic gripped his middle as he scanned flailing limbs and frantic faces. He pushed bodies aside, fighting toward where Bet had fallen.

A boot mashed his foot. An elbow met his nose. Still, he pressed.

Bang.

The crowd cleared out quicker after the second blast. He prayed the bullets he'd shot into the air didn't find a person when they came down. Unless it was that ragged hothead. He might deserve it.

Mercy, Lord God. Miss Leslie.

Terror twisted his middle. Sprawled face down at an odd angle, she'd been rolled several feet by the stampeding mob. A trail of blood followed. Her dark hair had torn loose of its bun and matted with sticky red against the visible side of her face. He gripped her shoulders and eased her over as gently as his gangly hands could manage. Her closed eyelids already tinted blue and purple.

"Miss Leslie—Bet—are you all right? Please, say something."

Dash it. He shouldn't have let this happen. But what could he have done? If it weren't for the Wobblies… She'd better wake up, or Denver might meet the equivalent of a witch-hunt. "Somebody, bring a doctor!"

No. He couldn't blame them completely. He'd been standing beside her the whole time. He should have stopped them. Anything to protect this innocent woman. He brushed the hair out of her face and placed a finger on her neck.

Thank God. A pulse, faint as it may be.

"Bet." Denny dropped to his knees beside Jasper. "Is she dead?"

Jasper pulled one hand away from her head. Sticky red coated his fingers. "Not yet, but we need to get her to a hospital—*now*."

The alarm bells clanged in the distance. Never did he think their signal of alarm would be welcome.

A whistle blew. Boots scuffled from behind. Then the constable bent down next to him.

Jasper glared. "Took you long enough. Where were you before this happened?"

Ignoring Jasper's comment, the constable fixed his gaze on Miss Leslie. "Is she the only one injured?"

Jasper opened his mouth to say yes, but the breath hitched in his chest. Mr. Rudin? He gripped Denny's shoulder. "Where's Mr. Rudin?"

The boy's frown deepened. "Last I saw him, inside."

His heart tore like the temple veil. He had to find Mr. Rudin. If the mob hadn't reached him, his own hand might. But how could he leave Miss Leslie unconscious and bleeding?

The clanging grew louder. Surely, the ambulance wouldn't be far behind.

He tightened his grip on Denny. "Stay with Miss Leslie. Don't leave her until she is safely in the ambulance. Understand?"

Denny nodded. "Promise."

With one last glance at the unconscious lady, Jasper stood and scanned the yard. Everything seemed a blur, but no figures besides Miss Leslie's lay on the ground. Mr. Rudin had to be inside.

"Mr. Rudin?" Jasper's call echoed down the empty hall. His long strides carried him to his employer's office, but the door hung ajar, the space empty. An eerie silence possessed the place.

He stepped inside, his gaze sweeping the room. Something was off. He approached the desk and the newspaper spread out on the surface. His jaw clenched.

RUDIN FACTORY HIDING CONTAMINATIONS.

Below the lying headline, they'd printed a Rudin Factory ledger. It listed dates and records of sugar tests finding contaminants of hair, dead rodents, and machine oil. Jasper's fingernails dug into his palms. McCracken would pay for this. But who was at the heart? He was beginning to think he knew. And he didn't like the answer.

He tucked the paper into his vest and whirled around. They

By Amber Schamel

had to uncover this quickly. December was their best month for sugar sales. They couldn't afford half production and lost contracts because of malicious interference.

A clanking from somewhere down the hall stiffened Jasper's shoulders. He followed the sound to Charlie bent over in the maintenance closet. "You're still here."

The janitor jumped, bumping his head on a shelf laden with soap and miscellaneous bolts and nuts. "Oh, detective, you startled me." He let out a nervous chuckle. "A factory as large as this one is creepy when silent."

"I would have expected you'd be gone, too."

"Nah, I'm not of any consequence to the Wobblies." He ran a hand through his gray mop of hair. "Besides, I can't afford to take any time off. Christmas is coming, you know. I have kiddies to buy for."

"True. Which begs the question as to why the workers were so upset about the night shift."

Charlie shrugged and reached for a mop. "Do you think they'll show up for the shift tonight?"

"I should think so. Things will be calm enough by then." Jasper crossed his arms and leaned against the doorjamb. "Did you hear which man squeaked?"

"Wish I did. The man deserves to be arrested for making such a fuss. And poor Mr. Rudin. The last couple of weeks are taking a toll on him, I think."

He had no idea. "Well, keep your ears open. If you hear anything, let me know."

"Will do." Charlie tossed a few tools into a box and then

135

traipsed down the hall.

"Oh, Charlie, did you happen to see to where Mr. Rudin was swept away to?"

"Can't say for sure. Mitch ushered him out the back door after you and Miss Leslie went outside. I heard Stosch say something about not taking him home. That's all I saw."

"Thanks." Jasper spun on his heel and marched toward the street. Stosch carted Mr. Rudin off to who-knows-where? He was getting a bad feeling about this whole business. He had to find the missing pieces before it was too late.

God, help me.

Chapter Thirteen

Jasper mounted the stairs onto the Rudin Mansion veranda two at a time. He slammed the lion head knocker five times. As soon as the doorknob turned, he pushed his way in. "Is Mr. Rudin at home?"

"No, sir. Only the misses."

"Where?" He strode down the hall, his slush-squishy soles slapping against the tile floor.

"Jasper? What's the matter?" Mrs. Rudin appeared at the top of the curved staircase.

"There's been trouble at the factory." He hesitated. "May we sit? I have some urgent questions."

Mrs. Rudin's face paled as she glided down the stairs. "Is Gustov all right?"

"I thought he would be here."

She pursed her lips and passed ahead of him toward the drawing room. After he entered, she closed the door. "What's this all about, Jasper?"

He clasped her frail hand in his and led her to the sofa. "Please sit down."

She obeyed, perching just on the edge of the flowery contraption, but Jasper couldn't bring himself to sit still. Instead, he paced in front of the marble hearth. The Christmas tree's piney scent engulfed him. It seemed everywhere he turned reminded him his time was running out.

"There was a protest at the factory today. The Wobblies. It grew violent for a few moments before they dispersed. One of our lady workers was injured. She's been taken to the hospital."

Mrs. Rudin twisted her hands in her lap, her right fingers pinching on her wedding band. "And Gustov?"

"Mitch and Stosch ushered him away. I don't know where he is."

"I see." Her light eyes seemed far away, and her lip trembled. "Then why do you have urgent questions?"

"Forgive me, Mrs. Rudin, you know I wouldn't ask such questions unless there was a real necessity, but I need to be frank."

She nodded and stroked her gray curls.

"Have you and Mr. Rudin been having difficulty?"

She lowered her eyes, like a child who knew they'd be found out. "We have seen better days, Jasper. I hate to say it, but we've become so distant over the years. He goes to the factory, and I wallow in what ifs and regrets."

"Some of his comments indicate arguments."

"It seems everything turns into one before long. I hate that factory of his. Every day I hate it more. And he loves it more than he loves me."

"Mrs. Rudin, you must know that can't be true."

She gave him a thin smile. "It isn't my food making him rounder every week. He survives on his sugar. It's been three months since we've dined together."

Three months? Jasper cleared his throat. "Mrs. Rudin, he still cares for you. He wants—"

"Cares? Yes. But care isn't enough to make a marriage happy. I can't expect you to understand such things, as a bachelor, but there is more to it than you know."

Oh, he'd bet there was.

Bet?

Was she all right? Had she awoken from the trauma?

Jasper shook his head to clear the thoughts. "He believes he cannot reclaim what he once had with you, though he wants to."

Mrs. Rudin crossed her arms and lifted her chin. "He's given up. That in itself is proof he doesn't care much at all."

"And you? Have you given up on him?"

Her eyes flashed as his question swatted her pride. "I am not the guilty party. You would understand that if you knew the entire story. It was Gustov who—oh, never mind. You men are all the same. But you just ask him. He'll tell you he's the one at fault."

Brilliant. Any time a woman got in a huff, they shut down. How did they manage to make everything impossible?

"I need to locate Mr. Rudin and speak to him immediately. Do you have any idea where Stosch and Mitch may have taken him?"

Shifting away from him, she tossed her hair over her shoulder. "How should I know? He never tells me anything."

Jasper stifled a growl and stomped toward the door. When he reached the front door, it swooshed open and nearly clobbered him. He jolted a step back.

"Jasper boy, what are you doing here?"

"Mr. Rudin?"

The elderly man chuckled as he set down his hat and coat. "Is it so surprising to find me at my own house?"

Apparently. If what his wife said was true.

"Are you all right, sir?"

Mr. Rudin raised one snowy brow. "I should be asking you. I was locked inside the factory for the duration."

"I'm dandy. It was Miss Leslie."

His eyes darkened. "My library. We can talk there." His gait was heavy as he trudged ahead.

"Gustov?" Mrs. Rudin trembled at the drawing-room door.

Her husband halted and pivoted partway. "Hello, my dear. Have a good morning?"

"I–I'm glad to see you're all right."

His jaw relaxed. "Thank you, Olivia. I will be out of your way as soon as the excitement abates." He gave her one of his lighthearted grins and proceeded down the hall.

Jasper tugged on his vest and followed, trying not to feel awkward at their exchange.

Mr. Rudin's library had always been Jasper's favorite room in the house. He'd spent hours there as a boy reading or studying his ship models and globes. The room didn't seem nearly so comfortable today. Accentuated by charcoal-gray walls, cherry wood furniture loomed dark and gloomy, casting shadows across the scarlet rug.

"How bad is Miss Leslie?" Mr. Rudin clasped his hands behind his back, facing the floor-to-ceiling bookshelf.

Jasper's throat went tight. If only he could answer with a positive! Instead, his gut tightened. "I'm not certain, sir. I was concerned for your safety, so I left her just before the ambulance arrived."

Rudin whirled around. "Ambulance? Was it so serious?"

"A rock connected with her head just before they rushed the door. She was unconscious."

"Trampled." Mr. Rudin braced both hands on the shelves. "This never should have happened. You should have let me go."

Jasper ventured a step forward. "They likely would have killed you."

"That would have been fine. What better way to die? I'd have gone down in the history books as a martyr for the capitalist cause. Now I'll be nothing more than a depressed old man who grew too weary of life's struggle."

"You can't do it. You can't throw your life away, Uncle Rudi." Did he sound as desperate as he felt? Maybe if he did, it would cause the man pause.

"Everything they say about me is true, Jasper. Did you hear? I am a tyrant. I do not know how to relate to my workers. I'm just a Russian man who fled to Denver looking to steal someone else's dream."

By Amber Schamel

"Someone else's? Whose dream was Rudin Sugar Company? Whose dream was Rudin Wing in the orphanage?"

Mr. Rudin shook his head, leaning even more on the bookcase. "Those things don't matter now. Every day I live, I end up doing more harm than good. Just think, if I had turned up dead this morning, the Wobblies never would have started the protest. Miss Leslie wouldn't be…in whatever shape she's in."

A pang shot through Jasper's stomach. "It's as much my fault as yours. I was right there. I should have protected her."

After a few heaving breaths, Mr. Rudin slammed his fist against the shelf. The books and trinkets rattled from the impact. More breathing. Then he straightened and walked to his desk. He placed one thick finger on the calendar. "December nineteenth. Just enough time for me to set things in order. I'll give God his full time. Five more days, but it's no use, Jasper."

Jasper bit down so hard his jaw shook. His face heated. And his fists clamped tight. He stalked toward the door. There, he stopped with a hand on the knob. "You're a selfish, stubborn, old codger, Uncle Rudi. Shame on you."

"Yes. Yes, I am. But don't worry. I'll not be a problem much longer."

By Amber Schamel

Chapter Fourteen

"How is she, doctor?" Jasper chomped hard on his lip as he stared at the fragile frame beneath a white sheet.

"I can't say for certain, detective. It's difficult to tell what internal injuries she sustained." The doctor checked his pocket watch. "I do hope she wakes soon. If she doesn't, the danger increases."

Jasper swallowed. Poor Miss Leslie—her face pale and bruised, her lips a light, purplish shade—looked nothing like a troll now. He didn't like the way they'd folded her dainty hands on her middle as if she were a fair maiden ready to be entombed. He picked up one hand and held it in his. No warmth. But at least, it wasn't stark cold. He laid it down at her side.

"If she doesn't improve?"

The doctor sighed. "We could try emergency surgery, but it is risky. If she's lost a lot of blood internally…" He trailed off as if not wanting to say the rest.

By Amber Schamel

"Has her family been contacted?" Jasper hated how that sounded. She couldn't die. Who would guard the bridge to Rudin Company?

"I understand she has a sister in the city. Your boy, Denny, went to fetch her."

At least his "sidekick" had done one thing right.

"You'd be proud of the kid. He was very protective of Miss Leslie. Bet, as he calls her. Wouldn't leave her side until she was situated, and only then to go for her sister."

Jasper pulled a card out of his pocket and flipped it to the doctor. "If her condition changes, please let me know. Rudin company will do all they can for her."

The doctor raised one blond eyebrow, but then shrugged. "Of course."

Swallowing hard this time, Jasper returned his gaze to Bet. How would the orphanage function without her? She shouldn't have stepped out those doors. It was stupid.

Liar. It was brave.

She must have felt some responsibility for the ruckus. Still, her pluckiness could have killed her. Could kill her. A heavy weight sank to the bottom of his stomach and settled like beet pulp at the bottom of a bucket. He hated nothing more than helplessness. He should leave. But what if no one was here when she did wake up? She deserved to have someone. Not to be alone after such a traumatic experience.

What was he thinking? He couldn't stay. How odd it would look for the company detective to stand nurse over an employee. And if she did awaken, she should see someone she didn't hate.

She'd probably blame him for the entire ordeal.

She had a right to. He winced, imagining her eyes fluttering open to see his duck lip and overbite looming over her. With his luck, he'd probably be muttering to himself or thinking deeply. His face always made idiotic expressions when he settled deep in thought.

Poor woman. Waking up alone would be better.

The thought propelled him out of the ward and out into the street.

*****

Jasper rolled over and shoved the clanging alarm clock onto the floor. A sharp thud and silence reigned once more. Some company should make one for folks like him with large, sensitive ears. The ticking, even from the floor, was enough to drive him mad. He shoved a pillow off the bed, but it did little to mute the sound.

He flung the cover aside but didn't get up. Saturday or no Saturday, he had a case to work. That was usually enough, but not today. Maybe if he let himself get cold, he'd get up and brew some coffee.

Why hadn't the doctor sent a message? Miss Leslie had to be conscious by now. Twenty-two hours had passed since her injury.

What if the clanging of his alarm drowned out the ringing of the doorbell? He jumped up and stumbled into the kitchen. He jerked open the door and stuck his head out, peering down the hall. "Hello?"

No one in sight, no message pinned on the door. But perhaps

the landlord's office had received a call. That would make more sense than sending a messenger. Smoothing his rumpled shirt, Jasper padded down the hall in sock feet. He nearly lost his balance trotting down the stairs to the first floor. Especially when his stocking feet met the lobby's marble tiling.

The clerk hardly looked up as he hunched over the ledgers. "May I help you?"

"Yes, Hollock from Apartment 259. Have I missed any calls?"

"No, sir. But I shall send for you directly if one should come in." The rough voice wasn't just froggy from the early hour.

"No need to be terse. I'm expecting an urgent call."

The clerk laid down his pen and pushed up the visor strapped around his dark head. "I assure you, Mr. Hollock, we wouldn't withhold an urgent call from you."

"Right. Well, it is urgent. And important."

"Yes, sir." The clerk followed him to the door and slammed it shut.

Jasper looked down at his black socks. He did look rather foolish. With a grunt, he shuffled back upstairs to the kitchen. He lifted the lid on the coffeemaker and measured out the grounds. Might as well put it on since he was already here. As the coffee percolated, he changed into clean clothes. The whistling of the pot lured him back. A thump outside his door signaled the arrival of the morning newspaper. He snatched it up and sat down with his coffee to see what McCracken had siphoned up today. He'd have that reporter's head on a platter as soon as he could prove the falsity of the reports.

By Amber Schamel

Woman Injured In Riot At Rudin Factory.

Jasper groaned. He couldn't read this. His gaze drifted to the date at the top, accented by Christmas wreaths. December 20. He only had a few days before Mr. Rudin would make the biggest mistake of his life.

And he had no idea how to stop him.

The familiar lead of helplessness plunged his stomach again, but this time, it mixed with an acidic roiling.

Failure.

His attempts seemed pitiful. He'd been so certain his plan would work. Now he was out of ideas…and out of time. The white sack that carried the hair into the factory lay crumpled on the table. He picked it up and turned it inside out. Hair flitted into his coffee cup. Jasper frowned. Blue thread?

The trill of the doorbell startled him. The doctor? He jerked the door open and startled the clerk. "A call for you, sir."

Jasper jogged ahead of him to the office and snatched up the receiver. "Detective Hollock speaking."

"Boss, it's Denny. I need you. Boiler room. This is the worst yet."

"I'll be right there." Jasper slammed down the receiver and brushed past the clerk. "Thanks." He bounded up the stairs to snag his coat, and then charged out the door. How did Denny get use of the company phone? And what was he doing at the factory on Saturday?

When Jasper reached the factory, his alarm tripled. Police, ambulance, and fire brigade? A pair of medical personnel descended the stairs.

By Amber Schamel

He caught one of them by the arm. "What's happened?"

"An accident with the night shift." He shrugged. "It's mostly cleaned up now."

"Anyone hurt?"

"Two. Third-degree burns, I'd guess. They were taken to the hospital."

Dash it all. Why hadn't someone called him sooner? Jasper released the medic and sprinted up the stairs two at a time. He veered toward the boiler room.

Denny stood in the doorway, his youthful face taut. "The night shift came on at nine o'clock. A few hours into their shift, the boiler machines broke belts and the buckets busted, leaking gallons of scalding liquid. Two of the men were burned bad. They took them to the hospital."

Jasper leveled a hard glare on the boy. "Why did you wait to call me?"

"Charlie and Mr. Rudin said you shouldn't be bothered. They'd clean up the mess, and there was nothing you could do anyway." Denny sniffed. "But I found something."

Spreading open his hands, Jasper gave an impatient shake of his head.

Denny tiptoed around the mess and slipped to the other side of the giant boiler. He picked up a black rubber belt and handed it to Jasper.

"A clean break."

The boy nodded. "Cut, I think."

He should have said "good eye", but he was too irritated to give any praise. Of course, this was done on purpose. And the sabotaging agent was getting more and more dangerous. "Details, people. Details. Haven't I drummed that into your thick skull yet? This is exactly why you should have called me." He threw down the belt and stepped closer to the machine and stuck his finger into a screw hole. Just as he feared. No tearing. The screws holding the metal sheets had been removed.

What would be next? If he didn't catch the traitor soon, someone was likely to die. If someone hadn't already.

The pieces were coming together, but not fast enough. Could Stosch have come to the factory after depositing Mr. Rudin at home? Possibly. After he'd been here with Charlie?

He didn't want to believe the conclusions logic and clues were throwing at him, but it was too dangerous to keep denying it. But what hard evidence did he have? Somehow, he had to get ahead and catch the culprit in the act.

"I've checked all of the windows, but they're locked." Denny strode to one and looked through. "I can't figure it out."

Jasper wasn't in the mood to explain endless possibilities. Especially when one seemed most probable. "Doors are much more convenient."

"But Charlie said he locked up after the riot and everyone left. I already asked him about it." The kid rocked back on his heels. "Unless they used the riot as a distraction while somebody slipped in and did the dirty work."

Exactly. But who would have known to plan on that? The answer was obvious. And there was nothing more infuriating than knowing who the culprit is and having no way to pin it on him.

By Amber Schamel

By Amber Schamel

Chapter Fifteen

Jasper inhaled sharply and turned. "I'm going to the hospital. I can't believe Miss Leslie hasn't woken yet, and I need to check on the two crewmembers."

"Oh, Miss Leslie woke up last night." Denny shrugged and flicked a dead bug from the windowsill. "She was talking, too. But she doesn't remember much."

Flexing his fingers and then curling them into fists, Jasper stepped forward. "How do you know?"

"The doctor rang up to the orphanage to let us know. Mrs. Yale and I went down right away to see her."

He could wring the kid's neck. Or he could wait and wring the doctor's. Why did it seem that everyone he gave explicit instructions to contact him did just the opposite? "Why didn't you call me?" The question sounded more like a growl, but it was becoming redundant. Something else that grated on his nerves.

151

Denny hopped a step back. "I didn't realize you'd want to know right away. Or that someone wouldn't have already told you."

"What are you? Errand and messenger boy? And aren't you the one who wanted to be my personal sidekick? But you can't even convey simple messages or urgent accidents? You're nothing more than a glorified gossip. I guess you think you're capable of solving the case yourself."

The kid's jaw clamped shut. And the mole on his right cheek ticked. "And you're nothing but a glorified bully. Shoving people around when you're nothing but a selfish, prideful despot. I thought you didn't need anyone's help?"

"I don't!"

"Fine! Then don't get mad at me for not pedaling you messages all day."

Their shouts echoed off the empty factory walls then faded into cold silence. Fists stiff at his sides, Jasper stalked toward the door.

"Wait."

Halting, Jasper braced.

"One last message. Mr. Rudin said to give you this." Denny shoved a piece of paper into his hand and then brushed past him.

Jasper unfolded the crumpled note.

Meeting with my lawyer Friday to finalize will. Come by my office Monday. I want to go over a few things before my last day.

His last day? As if Mr. Rudin were merely changing occupations. Jasper crunched the paper in his fist and tossed it into a trash bin as he passed the washroom. He finally had two cases. And both of them were ticking bombs, ready to explode and send Mr. Rudin and his empire crumbling to hell's ruins.

*****

The days seemed to drag by in a hazy blur. Dutifully checking in on Miss Leslie, but not having the heart to ask beyond how she felt. Checking in on the two burned men. Sunday. Church. Although the minister's words seemed to float in one ear and out the other this time. All they wanted to sing was Christmas hymns. Terribly distracting. He felt like a straw man, standing at his post, but having no heart or energy to put in. He even tried tinkering with his gadgets to free up his mental faculties, but the usual gimmick didn't work.

One thought kept running through his mind. Nothing. Nothing to offer Mr. Rudin. Nothing to stop the man bent on destroying him. Today he would go over the will with Mr. Rudin. Less than three days till Christmas. This was his last chance, and he still had nothing to say.

He trudged up the steps and veered toward Mr. Rudin's office.

"Hollock." Stosch straightened his monocle and pinned him with a sharp gaze. "What about this case?"

Jasper blinked. "Case?" How would Mr. Stosch know about either one?

"Perhaps you've been hiding in a cave, but everyone else hasn't. The papers have been raving about sabotage. That has to be what you've been occupied with."

Should he tell Stosch he's one of his prime suspects? "I'm very close to a conclusion, Mr. Stosch. But it's classified

153

information. Is Mr. Rudin prepared to see me?"

"He's been asking after you all afternoon."

"Don't bother getting up. I'll see myself in."

Jasper tapped on the door with a knuckle before opening. Mr. Rudin was bent over papers scattered across his desk. "There you are, Jasper boy. I was wondering if Denny hadn't delivered my note."

"Haven't you seen him?"

"Not since Saturday. Mr. Stosch said he's out looking for another job."

Jasper swallowed. That had to be his fault. "Anyway, you wished to see me?"

"Sit down. This will take a while."

He settled into the leather chair and crossed one leg over his knee and his arms across his chest.

"A few portions of this will concern you, my boy. As you know, you're not just my detective, but more like the son I never had. So I've treated you as such in my will. Everything goes to my wife, of course, but I leave you as coexecutor. I've also made a few requests."

"So you're leaving me money in place of a father?"

A gentle smile curled beneath Mr. Rudin's mustache. "I figured your mood wouldn't be bright, but in the long run, you'll appreciate it."

Jasper bit down on the inside of his cheek. Scenes of his mother's funeral oozed into his mind.

"I've left instructions regarding the orphan program you proposed, as well as the continuance of the factory. Although, it seems there's not much left for you to salvage." Mr. Rudin picked up a stack of papers and tossed them across the desk. "Those are from our largest clients. They have great concerns about our quality and ability to fulfill orders. They've been loyal to me for years, but without proof of the foul play, I have nothing to counter with."

Closing his eyes, Jasper took in a deep breath, willing the tears burning to disappear. He felt like a little boy all over again, about to lose the person who meant the world to him. He had one last plea to try. "Uncle Rudi, if you take your own life, I'll do the same."

For a split second, hesitation flashed in the man's blue eyes. Then he chuckled. "Your eye is twitching."

Unless he was lying to himself, the words were true. Regardless of his stupid twitch. "I can't stand the loss. Not again. When Mother died, I had you. But if you go, I have no one."

"One look at my wife with tears in her eyes, and you'll change your mind. She has a way with men and tears." Mr. Rudin sat back with a sigh. "Make sure when she remarries it's a good man."

Jasper couldn't stand it anymore. Like a feral rat from a house aflame, he bolted.

*****

Jasper fell to his knees, dampness seeping through his trousers. His mother's white marble headstone was nearly invisible in all the snow. Hand shaking, he reached out and brushed away the fluff to reveal her name. Mary Jane Hollock.

By Amber Schamel

The most beautiful name ever etched in stone. His body trembled, but the cold wind or dampness didn't cause it.

"Mother, I wish you were here. You'd know what to do."

She would. But he'd never want her to see him like this.

"He's going to do it. And I have no way to stop him." Bowing his head, he sucked in a breath. "Then there's the sabotage."

He wanted to say more, but he was too worn out to rehash the frustration and hopelessness. Talking to a tombstone wouldn't help anyway. Sitting back on his haunches, he brushed hair from his eyes. Here he thought he was such an unnoticed gem. A mastermind only needing an opportunity. Hmmph. Denny was right. And his own pride made him scoff at himself. He'd managed to mess everything up in a matter of weeks.

This needed to stop. He sounded like Mr. Rudin.

Oh well. He'd end up beside him in less than thirty-six hours. He squeezed his eyes shut against the image of Mr. Rudin lying in a puddle his office floor, Jasper picking up the gun to follow suit.

Perhaps Mr. Rudin was right after all. Every bit of suffering, disappointment, and work that went into everyday life was worth nothing in the end. All vanity as Ecclesiastes says.

The wind whisked snow across the grave in front of him. "What am I missing?"

The key.

The words stamped his heart as if whispered from heaven. Mother had always told him prayer was the key that opened locked doors and unleashed the floodgates of heaven. His chin

By Amber Schamel

met his chest as shame heated his face. Here he called himself a Christian, but in the midst of confusion, he ran to his mother's grave to try to talk to her instead of talking to the God he believed was alive. The story of Saul calling Samuel from the grave rose in his memory.

"God, forgive me." His whispered breath hung in the air between him and his mother's name. "I've been seeking help in the wrong place, and I've wound up at the same dead end as Mr. Rudin." He paused, giving his heart time to open up to the Holy Spirit. "But I'm not the same as Mr. Rudin, am I?"

No. As much as he wanted to think he would lay himself out beside the man, Jasper could never do it. Why? Was he a coward? Was it because he'd be swayed by Mrs. Rudin's tears as Uncle Rudi had said?

Jasper shook his head. It was something deeper. He couldn't end his own life because he felt deep inside that he would be throwing it away. That there was more to accomplish. His life was still worth living.

"But why, Lord? What makes it worth living? What makes mine different from Mr. Rudin's?"

Walk with me.

Rising, Jasper brushed off the snow. He followed the Holy Spirit's prompting and strolled toward the cemetery entrance. Passing the portico of the cemetery office, he kept his heart and mind quiet, listening for the still, small voice.

Birds flitted across the park, chirping as they went. Clumps of snow fell from burdened trees as he passed. The city noise increased as he neared the street. He paused at a corner to listen

By Amber Schamel

to a school choir sing "God Rest Ye Merry Gentlemen" before he continued across the street toward downtown.

"Let nothing you dismay. Remember Christ our Savior…." He certainly felt dismayed. Perhaps his thoughts had been too occupied to let him think on the right things.

Hands pocketed against the frigid air, he walked for a long time in silence, his steps carrying him closer to the factory and Union Station. Holiday travelers thronged the cars, luggage everywhere. Fancy electric string lights illuminated Merry Christmas on the side of a wall. The blaring of the train whistles and the hum of crowds overtook the peaceful silence he'd enjoyed earlier.

All right, God, how am I to hear You now?

"Some say God is so hard to find, so difficult to hear, but God is all around us. Especially during this season." A strong, low voice carried through the crowd, echoing off the station's stone walls. "In our darkest moments, He is there, ready and willing to help if only we would ask."

I have asked, Lord.

Peering through the people filing by, Jasper tried to identify the voice. He pressed toward it.

"When you feel like you've come to a dead end, He brings a new beginning."

The voice grew louder with each step Jasper took, but he couldn't see the source.

"When your life is no longer worth living, when you're washed up with nothing left, give your life to Christ, and He will give you His. What an exchange that is, my friend! Because He

158

lives, our lives have meaning. Perhaps you've believed there is no reason. There is no hope. But Christ died to give you a different path."

Jasper pressed against one of the walls as a cart laden with suitcases trundled past. Then he caught sight of a man standing on the platform's edge, holding a Bible above his head. "It's not what you do, friend, that makes your life worth living. Not our own works, for the Bible tells us those are as filthy rags. But it is the life of Christ—what He makes us—that gives us purpose and meaning. His vision of us as sons and daughters of God."

Was someone hammering the other side of the wall, or was it his own heartbeat? The preacher's gaze locked with Jasper's, and the buzz around him faded, leaving nothing but his own breathing.

The man's voice lowered, as did the Bible above his head. "This is how we face our trouble. It's the life behind the name of Jesus Christ."

The words addressed Mr. Rudin's issue perfectly. Why then, did Jasper feel like a child squirming beneath a reproachful stare?

"Not our works. Not what others say we are. Not what we say we are. But what the King of Heaven and Earth says we are. You may say you're a failure. Others may agree. But Christ says you're worth everything, and His is the judgment that counts."

Jasper's hands trembled against the cold stone wall as a warmth spread through his chest. He bowed his head and squeezed his eyes shut. Hot tears burned the inside of his eyelids. Avoiding the street preacher's gaze, he slipped through

By Amber Schamel

the crowd and trotted toward home. His hands still shook when he inserted the key in his apartment lock.

He slammed the door behind him and stalked to his mirrors. Staring at his glowering reflection, he heard his own words played back again.

Seeing his perspective in God's looking glass, he saw the end of his path merge with Mr. Rudin's. Perhaps he had begun slightly different, but the end was the same. He'd been so focused on his career, on making a name for himself, that he'd allowed it to define him. Pride would be his downfall. Whether he met his self-imposed expectations or not, it would be a dead end. The value of his life, his reason for living would disappear.

But he knew better. How was it so easy to forget?

"Lord God, am I really worth so much to You?" Falling to his knees, Jasper prayed. Not like he prayed every night, but like a gush of water released from an overfilled dam. By the time he opened his eyes, he could hardly see. When had it gotten dark? He reached over and tugged on the lamp switch. His eyes, swollen and red, made his reflection a ghastly sight, but he couldn't help but grin. A flame had ignited inside his heart, and with it, an excitement for what the future may hold. No, he wouldn't end up like Mr. Rudin. Not for the same reason he thought before, but because of Christ.

He stared at his reflection and blinked. Poor Uncle Rudi. Tomorrow was his last chance, but this time, Jasper knew what needed to be said.

By Amber Schamel

Chapter Sixteen

Jasper's step was light as he entered the factory. He mounted the stairs two at a time, pausing for breath at the top. *Lord, give me the words to get this across to Uncle Rudi.*

"Good morning, Stosch. May I have a few moments with Mr. Rudin?"

The secretary adjusted his monocle as he lifted one brow. "What's this? Did Detective Hollock just address me in a civil manner? Perhaps I should call the nurse."

If he hadn't promised himself he'd be polite, Jasper would have rolled his eyes and dished out a spicy retort. Instead, he forced a smile. "I'll assume that means his morning calendar is clear." He took a step toward the door.

"Mr. Rudin isn't in yet."

Jasper frowned and pulled out his pocket watch. "It's a quarter to nine."

Stosch sucked in a breath. "So you can tell time."

"Did you see him leave last night?" Jasper stepped behind the secretary's chair and picked up the receiver on the candlestick telephone. He gave the hook a few taps. "Hello? Operator, ring the residence of Gustov Rudin right away, please."

"One moment, sir." You'd think telephone operators lived in some far away cave.

Jasper tapped his foot as he waited. "Well, Stosch? Did you see him leave?"

"No, I left before him last night."

Unease slithered up Jasper's neck. He stared at the brass knob on Mr. Rudin's office door. Was it locked? What would he find if it wasn't?

"Hello?" Mrs. Rudin's voice filtered through the line.

"Mrs. Rudin, this is Jasper. Is your husband still at home?"

"What? Is he not there? He was already gone when I woke this morning."

The toast Jasper had for breakfast morphed to acid in his stomach. "Was he at home for dinner?"

"No, he phoned and said he'd be working late and not to worry."

"Thank you, ma'am. I'll call you back." He slammed the receiver down before she could ask more questions. His stomach churned as he faced the door.

The knob burned like ice beneath Jasper's grasp. His left hand turned while his right knuckle rapped on the door. "Mr. Rudin?"

No answer. Jasper's nerves tensed as the door eased open

By Amber Schamel

under his pressure. He held his breath and peered inside. "Sir?"

The papers strewn about the desk were a bad omen. Uncle Rudi never left without clearing his desk for the next day. But there was no blood. That much was good. Jasper stepped into the room and caught sight of a hand on the far side of the floor. "Oh, God, please."

His voice must have carried urgency because Stosch was suddenly right behind him as he rushed around the desk. Mr. Rudin lay sprawled out on the floor, dried blood caking his head.

"He must have hit the bookcase when he fell." Stosch's voice trembled.

Jasper knelt and placed two fingers to the man's neck. "He's alive. Call for an ambulance."

*****

Jasper stood and stretched his aching back. What time was it? He'd offered to sit beside Mr. Rudin overnight so the missus could get some rest. Poor woman had been panic-stricken by the time Jasper went to break the news. Apparently, whatever ailment Mr. Rudin suffered during the night caused a nasty fall. The doctor's prognosis wasn't bright. If he pulled through, severe complications were imminent. Memory loss, paralysis, and a lot of other big words that sent Mrs. Rudin back into hysteria.

If it weren't so serious, Jasper would have hoped he lost the memory of his desire for suicide.

"Please, God." Jasper folded his hands and leaned against the mattress as he whispered those words for the hundredth time. "Let him pull through. Give me a chance to share what You

By Amber Schamel

showed me. If it's Your will to take him, fine. But please let me speak to him first."

Speak to him now.

Faint light from the hall lamps shadowed Mr. Rudin's motionless features. Without his half-smile beneath it, his mustache hung oddly against pasty-white skin. Could it be that Mr. Rudin's desire to die was keeping him from recovering?

Jasper checked his pocket watch. Midnight. That made it Christmas Eve. Only hours until Mr. Rudin's self-appointed rendezvous with death.

Resolve coursed through Jasper's veins. Straightening, he glanced around, but the hospital row was quiet, no nurses in earshot. "Uncle Rudi? Can you hear me?" He pursed his lips as he waited, but he wasn't going to let a lack of response deter him. "I've solved your case."

It might have been imagined. Or Mr. Rudin's snowy eyebrow may have really twitched.

"I've enlisted some help. You were right. You are a hard case. But I've found one who has never lost one."

This was almost as crazy as talking to his mirrors. Oh well, that never stopped him before.

"There's one thing you've overlooked. You said you're hopeless, that nothing can change, there's no point in going on. But what you didn't know is there is Someone who will change you. Someone who brings hope. Someone who gives you a future and makes life worth living again. I know you've heard His name, but you've never met Him in person. If you'd wake up, I'd like to introduce you."

By Amber Schamel

"I've met Jesus, Jasper boy." The man's hoarse voice startled him. "Remember? That's the whole reason I assigned the case to you."

Relief flooded Jasper's body, and breathing became easier. "I know that, sir, but there's a difference in being acquainted and being best friends."

Mr. Rudin winced and reached for his head. "Is that supposed to turn on a light in my brain like some fandangled electric switch?"

"Well, yes, in a way. Uncle Rudi, what sin do you regret the most tonight?"

"Going to make me rehash that, are you?" He dragged a hand across his face and sighed. "I suppose there's no harm in telling it now."

Jasper nodded.

"When I was young, we moved from Russia to New York. I lived down the street from the most beautiful girl in the world. When I finally got her to notice me, I gave everything I had to winning her. But our parents didn't agree with the match. Mine wanted me to marry a Russian, and hers just didn't like me. So we eloped."

Giving in to his numb knees, Jasper lifted himself back to the chair beside Mr. Rudin's bed. "And that's what is causing you guilt?"

"No." Mr. Rudin tipped his head back, his eyes catching the lamplight and giving him a faraway look. "We needed something to make a start. Both of our families had good money, and they would have given us a stake, had they agreed. So, in

165

my foolish youth, I decided they owed it to us regardless. I convinced Olivia to take from her parent's safe, and I took from mine. When we got to Denver, I used the money to start Rudin Company."

Jasper blinked. "You and Mrs. Rudin stole from your parents?"

The elder man's lips pressed into a fine line. "I can't even apologize and make it right. Both sets of parents passed away years ago." He shut his eyes and leaned back. "Olivia has never forgiven me."

"You may not be able to ask your parents' forgiveness, but Christ is ready to grant His."

"What difference will that make? It wasn't His money we stole."

"What would it hurt to give it a try?"

Mr. Rudin sighed. "My head hurts. Will you help me?"

Leaning forward, Jasper laid a hand on his arm. "It's easy. No rituals or recitations. Just speak the same way you would to your wife or your parents if they were still alive."

The elder man shifted, his eyes squinting as he pressed them shut. "God? Or Jesus…" He opened his eyes a slit and cast a questioning glance at Jasper. After Jasper's quick nod of reassurance, Mr. Rudin closed his eyes again. "It's been many years, but I did wrong. I have no idea how it hurt my parents or if it caused them hardship, but they're gone now. Or I would have repented to them first. But I am sorry, and I'm in need of forgiveness. Jasper says that's something You can give to me, so I'm asking You. Please forgive me. Let this black mark over my

166

life release me and help me find a way to repair the damage it's done."

Jasper studied Mr. Rudin's face. Deep wrinkles in the man's forehead came from more than just age. He'd carried this guilt for so long—no wonder his burden seemed unbearable. But as the prayer drifted from his parched lips, the lines ironed out and his face relaxed.

"And, God, while You're at it, if You can pardon me from all my many sins, I'm ready to get rid of them."

The words stopped, but Mr. Rudin's eyes remained closed. His breath wheezed out of his lungs in long heaves. At last, he opened his eyes. "I do feel different."

"Yeah." Jasper smiled. "Happens to me, too."

"I think He really heard me."

A chuckle escaped. "Of course, He did. God has big ears. That's where I get mine."

Mr. Rudin laughed then, but it ended in a wince. "My head aches."

"You took a nasty fall. Do you remember what happened?"

A frown brought the wrinkles back. "Something bad happened at the factory. We're not making enough."

"What else do you remember?"

"I–I don't know. Where is Olivia?"

"Home, I sent her for some rest."

The frown lines deepened as he looked around the room. The faint light from the lamps at the end of the hall didn't paint much of a picture, but his gaze lingered on the bedside tray. "I'm not at home. Is this the hospital?"

By Amber Schamel

"Yes, sir. You worked late last night and collapsed. The doctor thinks it was an apoplexy. At any rate, we didn't find you until the next morning. You're lucky to be alive."

"Is that why I can't move my legs?"

A shot of alarm coursed up Jasper's chest. "You can't move them?" He stood and squeezed the man's ankle. "Can you feel this?"

Mr. Rudin shook his head.

Jasper moved to the other ankle. "This one?"

"No."

Dash it. If he couldn't feel, he certainly couldn't walk. How long would it take for him to gain it back? "I'll call the doctor."

Mr. Rudin waved at the chair. "No, no. We'll worry about that later. Sit down and tell me what's been going on at the factory. My memory is foggy, but I know there was something wrong."

With a glance at the door, Jasper relented. The doctor would be around soon enough, and it wouldn't be right to leave Uncle Rudi alone in the dark while he was awake.

Jasper returned to the chair. "You remember telling me about your deal with God?"

"I don't think I could forget the expression on your face." Mr. Rudin chuckled.

"What do you remember after that?"

Rudin shrugged, his mouth puckering in a wince.

That left a lot to fill in. Jasper gave him a summary of the past few weeks, right up to when he'd sent Mrs. Rudin home a few hours before. "And that brings us up to the early hours of

By Amber Schamel

Christmas Eve. It's a bit past two."

"Christmas." Mr. Rudin's eyes misted over. "Can we have Christmas in a hospital?"

"Of course, we can. What do you want? Presents? Turkey dinner?"

Mr. Rudin's mustache twitched beneath his familiar grin. "A snowman."

Jasper laughed. "I'll see what I can do."

"What about you, Jasper boy? What do you want for Christmas?"

Leaning back, Jasper laced his fingers behind his head and stretched. "I want to solve this case and catch the crook responsible for all this."

"Then go do it."

"If it were so easy, it'd be done. I have no hard evidence to pin him with."

"That's the key, isn't it?" Mr. Rudin sighed and weathered the edge of the sheet.

The key.

Why did those words keep emerging in his mind? He must really need to pray more. He rubbed his fingers together. "Yes, if only I had a master key to solve every case."

"Master keys are quite something, aren't they? I've never had so much fun as when the locksmith came to the factory last year. He could make keys fit as many doors as I wanted them to. Kendall has a key that opens the lab and the back door. Stosch has one that opens most doors. Charlie got one that opens almost everything. But my key opens every lock in that place."

By Amber Schamel

Jasper's fingers stilled. "What does Charlie's key not open?"

"My locked closet in the corner of my office is about the only thing."

Chewing his cheek, Jasper ran through clues. "Is your key still in your office?"

"It never leaves."

Jasper's heart rate picked up. Perhaps the key he needed was there after all.

Chapter Seventeen

The bloodstain still marred the carpet when Jasper entered Mr. Rudin's office. Hadn't Stosch called Charlie in to clean up?

Maybe it was better that he hadn't.

"Stosch, when do all the workers leave for the holiday?"

The elderly secretary peeked through the doorway. "In about thirty minutes. Mr. Rudin gave them a half-day off. Why?"

"That should be sufficient time." After depositing his coat on a chair, Jasper bit his cheek and scanned the room. The locked filing cabinet on the left-hand side of the room was mostly hidden by Mr. Rudin's desk and window drapes. He turned around and placed one hand on the door. "Excuse me for a moment, Stosch, I have something to look into for Mr. Rudin."

Jasper shut the door and crossed to the backside of the desk. He opened the hidden drawer and pulled out the key. RSF—the same engraving as he'd seen before—etched the surface. He grasped it firmly between his fingers and stepped to the locked

171

cabinet. He pushed the key into the lock. So far, it fit. He twisted, but the lock didn't turn. Reversing directions, it still didn't budge.

This was exactly what he'd been praying for.

"Where's Mr. Rudin?"

Jasper started at Denny's voice from the doorway. He whirled around to see the boy standing, arms crossed, with his brows drawn low. "Denny, glad you're here."

One eyebrow quirked up. "I'm here to give my notice to Mr. Rudin. Where is he?"

"Notice?" This time, it was Jasper's turn to scowl.

"That's right. The position I've found at the pharmacy pays more."

Brilliant. He'd almost forgotten about their spat earlier. Denny must still be upset about it. "We'll talk about that later. Right now, I need your help."

Denny spread his feet farther apart and raised his chin. "And why should I help you?"

Jasper released an impatient sigh. "Because Mr. Rudin is in the hospital and I'm about to solve the case. Now do you want to go home, or are you going to help me?"

The boy's hands dropped to his sides, even as his mouth fell open. He took a step closer, his eyes sweeping the bloody spot on the floor. "Is Mr. Rudin all right?"

"Time will tell. Hand me my coat."

Denny picked up the black wool jacket and held it out. "The blood is his?"

Jasper nodded as he reached into his coat pocket. "I'll

172

explain later." His fingers met with the cool metal of his newest contraption. He'd fiddled with it during those torturous hours of the past week when he could neither sleep nor come up with answers, and now he was glad he had. This would be the perfect opportunity to test them. He stuck one arm in the coat, winked at Denny, and then shoved his other arm into it, knocking over a bottle on Mr. Rudin's drink table in the process. "Dash it, clumsy me. I've spilled some of Mr. Rudin's drink. Mr. Stosch, would you be so good as to call Charlie in to clean up this mess?"

"I can—" Jasper halted Denny's offer with an upheld palm.

Stosch's monocle fell from his eye as he looked over Denny's shoulder. "Really, detective, someone with your…" He cleared his throat. "*Skill*…shouldn't be so clumsy. Isn't it your job to be observant?"

"So it is. Are you going to call Charlie?"

"Fine."

Denny lifted his hands in a question when the secretary walked away.

"In case I am wrong—which I won't be—I didn't want him to overhear. I'm about to arrest the man responsible for the sabotage incidents. If my contraption malfunctions, don't let him get out that door and try not to let him hurt you." Jasper pulled back his coat to indicate the pistol shoved in his waistband. "I'll shoot him if I have to."

The kid's eyes were big as Stosch's pride and Jasper's put together. "Details, Denny. Details. You're about to witness their power."

173

Footsteps approached, and soon the secretary appeared with the janitor on his heels.

"There you are, Charlie. I've made a horrible mess in here, would you help me clean it up?" Jasper grabbed a napkin from the table and bent down to mop up some of the liquid.

"That's what I'm here for, cleaning up everyone else's mess." Charlie yanked a rag from his belt and stooped beside Jasper.

Slipping one hand into his coat pocket, Jasper grasped his gadget. When Charlie reached out to dab the wet spot, Jasper slung the altered handcuffs out of his pocket and clamped them on the man's wrists before he could recoil.

"Hey! What are you doing? Binding the hands that clean for you is akin to biting the hand that feeds ya." Charlie's brown eyes creased at the sides with an easy smile.

"Except when those are the hands that harm the man that feeds you."

The janitor laughed. "You've gone too many hours without sleep, detective. Take these off, and I'll fix you a cup of coffee."

Jasper yanked the keys from Charlie's side. He singled out the master he'd seen before as he made his way to the cabinet. He inserted the key and rotated.

Click.

Jasper met Stosch's and Denny's befuddled gazes. "Gentlemen, I present to you the culprit. Mr. Perkins is under arrest for charges of sabotage, defamation, and tampering in the first degree with intent to harm."

Stosch straightened his monocle. "Him?"

"But…I thought…" Denny pointed to Stosch, then to Charlie as perplexity wrinkled his brow. "The Wobblies?"

"Not the Wobblies as we originally thought." Jasper turned back to the janitor. "Perhaps you would like to explain how you came to be mixed up in all this mess?"

Charlie shook his head, strands of gray hair slapping his face. "I don't know what you're talking about."

"No? Then tell me how Mr. Rudin's key came to be on your ring."

"It's a master key. I told you as much the night you found the key under the crystallizing machine."

Jasper couldn't help the smug grin inching across his face. He looked to Denny, who was rocking back and forth on his heels, squinting at him.

"You didn't ever tell Charlie where you found the key. You just asked to see his."

"Brilliant, Denny. You were paying attention to the details."

The boy's fingers went to his chin. "So, how did you know it was him?"

"I didn't want to believe it was you, Charlie. I truly didn't. But soon it became too sure to deny." Jasper held up one finger. "First, the mess in the laboratory. You claimed the spill happened during the break-in, but if it had been hours since the spill, it wouldn't have needed a mop. Your shoes were sticky from the sugar water, which indicated the spill had been recent and you had tracked through it. That also explained why the mop trail went to the window and to the door. You were covering your tracks."

By Amber Schamel

Charlie clamped his mouth shut.

Jasper lifted a second finger. "Each incident could only have been perpetrated by someone with a key since no tampering or breaking in was evident. I became more suspicious when the newspaper reported details on the hair contamination that only the three of us would have known."

Stosch clicked his tongue. "Now wait a moment, someone who did the deed would have details on the mess."

"True, but not details on the cleanup as well." Lifting a third finger, Jasper stepped closer to Charlie. "When the machines mysteriously broke down, you just happened to be around with a wrench to match the missing nuts, which I spotted in your janitor closet later."

Charlie's hands fisted in the cuffs. "None of that is enough to pin such serious accusations on me, Hollock. You're in a mad guessing game."

"Fourth, you were the only person in the factory after the riot and before the night shift when the machines fell apart. Fifth, and most confirming of my suspicions, is the key."

"The key is mine. It proves nothing more than my occupation as janitor. A fact you should know well. This whole thing is ridiculous. I am the one who alerted you to the break-in and incidents, yet you blame me?"

"You had a sack of hair dumped into the machine when you heard Denny and me coming. In your rush, you dropped your key. Fortunately for you, you heard it drop and knew it would be a sure way of getting caught if you didn't have your key in a matter of minutes when I called on you, so you went to Mr.

Rudin's office to get his."

"You can't prove it's not my key." The janitor's face turned red as a streetcar. His Adam's apple bobbed.

"I can." Jasper reached into his coat pocket, pulled out the blue-threaded sack, and bent to Charlie's level. "The only thing left for you to tell us is how much Wiles Sugar paid you, Judas."

"I've worked for Rudin year after year, and he's never given me anything more than a pat on the back and ham for Christmas. Wiles offered me a management position, something I could never attain here."

"Well, you've attained a jail cell for sure, and if you ever get released, I doubt anyone other than the devil himself would hire you."

Charlie jerked his wrists away and let out a yelp.

"Don't make a fuss. These handcuffs have spring-released pins activated by sudden movement. And the acid injected by the pins will burn more with increased body heat. The more you struggle, the more pain."

With a strong finger on either side of Charlie's neck, Jasper lifted him to his feet. "Stosch, ring down to the station and have the police come pick him up. We'll need both you and Denny to sign witness statements." He paused beside Denny and lowered his voice. "If I let you ride in the paddy wagon, can we be friends again?"

The dimple appeared on Denny's cheek. "Is that as close to an apology as I'm gonna get?"

"Don't push it, kid."

"All right, I'll take it. You better be glad your sidekick is so forgiving."

With his free hand, Jasper spread his palm over the boy's cap and gave it a whirl.

By Amber Schamel

Chapter Eighteen

"So old Charlie did all this to me?"

The betrayal in Uncle Rudi's voice was painful. Jasper sighed. "Well, at least we caught him."

"The poor man will be spending Christmas in jail." Mr. Rudin reached over and tapped the notebook on Jasper's lap. "Tell Stosch I want to send his family dinner and some gifts for the children."

There was no end to the kindness in this man's heart. Jasper jotted down the note and looked up. "That covers Mrs. Rudin's gift, what you want brought down for the day, and Charlie's family. Anything else?"

A mischievous twinkle lit in the old man's eye. "Yes, Jasper must ask Miss Leslie to join him for Christmas dinner. Whether she gets released today or not."

One of Jasper's brows quirked up. "Are you ordering me to ask her for a date?"

By Amber Schamel

Uncle Rudi grinned and folded his arms across his chest. "Somebody's got to, or you'll be a grumpy bachelor forever."

"I think Denny's bending your ear."

Jasper stood, but Mr. Rudin grasped his sleeve. "Write it on your list, Jasper Hollock, or I'll fire you by Monday."

Dash it. Why was everyone so determined to see him hitched? He sat back down, took a deep breath, and rested his fists on the notebook. "Tell you what, we'll make a deal. If you will take your wife out on a date, romance her the way you did back in New York, then I will ask Miss Leslie to join us for Christmas dinner in the hospital lounge."

"Done."

"But you have to treat Mrs. Rudin gallantly. Expensively."

Uncle Rudi picked up the newspaper from the side table and swatted Jasper's arm. "I said I'll do it, now get over there and ask Miss Leslie."

Heat already crept up Jasper's neck, but he stood and shoved the notebook under his arm. "Fine."

He stalked down the rows of beds and toward the south wing. It wasn't likely Bet would still be in hospital tomorrow, and even if she was, it would be a friendly and cordial gesture to ask her to join them. Hardly a date.

Or would Miss Leslie see right through that facade? He wasn't sure if he wanted her to or not.

Jasper stepped into the ward and immediately spotted her. She was sitting up, her long brown hair falling around her shoulders as she focused on the nurse and Denny at the end of her bed. Her hazel gaze flickered to him as he approached.

"If you follow those instructions closely, you shouldn't have any complications. But be careful not to overdo yourself through the holiday, Miss Leslie." The nurse gave her a firm glare.

"At this point, I'm just glad to be home for Christmas. I'll be good."

"Mrs. Yale will make better on that promise than your patient, nurse." Denny bent his head toward her. "But you can be sure she'll be in good hands."

"Very well, then. Here are your discharge papers. I assume someone will be picking you up?"

"Mrs. Yale will be around shortly. Thank you."

Jasper smiled at Bet as the nurse walked away. She clutched the bedsheet as a clamped-lip smile held in her excitement. "Breaking free of here, are you?"

"Thanks to Mrs. Yale's offer to look after me for a couple of weeks while I recover."

He grasped the iron bed frame. "What about your sister? Don't relatives usually do that sort of thing?"

"Of course, they do." Miss Leslie crossed her arms and leveled her green-tinted gaze at him. "Georgie would love to, but her small house is already filled with children. She wouldn't have room for me."

Something about her answer didn't sit right, but Jasper decided to let it slide. Wouldn't be wise to get into an argument when he was about to ask her to dinner. "I was going to ask if you'd like to join us for Christmas dinner. The Rudins are arranging for a special meal in the lounge for the occasion."

"How kind of them to think of me."

Jasper cleared his throat and tried to avoid Denny's stupid grin and teasing eyes. "Well, I hoped it would cheer you up if for some reason you didn't get to go home."

Miss Leslie tipped her head and squinted at him from the corner of her eye. "That…was thoughtful…I suppose."

She supposes. Women are insufferable.

"Unfortunately, I'll have to decline. The kids at the orphanage visited yesterday, and I promised them I'd be there before the stockings were filled."

"Well, we wouldn't want to disappoint them, would we?" He let go of the bed frame and stepped back, hoping his ears weren't as red hot as they felt.

Denny's snort said they were.

"Of course, if you aren't too busy after your dinner with Mr. Rudin, you could always stop by the orphanage. The children would love to have a detective to bombard with questions. And I could do with some mature conversation by the end of the day."

A grin tugged at the corners of his mouth. "Well now, Miss Leslie, I think that's the nicest string of words you've ever said to me. But, I wonder, could that be considered a date?"

She tilted her head and rested her index finger on her chin. "Mmm, no. Definitely not a date."

"Oh." The urge to grin disappeared.

"I thought about it, though." She lifted one shoulder, and the gold speck in her eye glinted. "Only for a split second, but that is something considering I hated you last week." Her chuckle— almost a giggle—lightened the blow.

Jasper flashed Denny a grin. "Something, indeed. Well, my

pride is wounded, but at least I have 'something' to work with."

Denny tipped his head back and let out a hearty laugh. "You bet."

The End

Thank you for reading!

Thank you so much for joining me on Jasper's adventure! If you enjoyed *Solve by Christmas* please consider leaving a review, sharing with your friends on social media, or requesting it at your local library.

If we haven't met, I'd love to make your acquaintance! I love meeting and talking to other readers and lovers of history. You can find me on my website, http://www.Amberschamel.com, or at any of the following:

Sign up for our Newsletter and get a Short Story FREE!

Blogs - http://stitchesthrutime.blogspot.com/
http://www.hhhistory.com/
http://amberschamel.blogspot.com/

Facebook - https://www.facebook.com/AuthorAmberSchamel

Twitter - @AmberSchamel https://twitter.com/AmberSchamel

Pinterest - http://pinterest.com/AmberDSchamel/

Goodreads -
https://www.goodreads.com/author/show/7073165.Amber_Schamel

More by Amber Schamel

Excerpt from The Swaddling Clothes

Chapter One

Circa 980 B.C.

King David drummed his fingers on the arm of his throne. The merchant's monotone voice had been echoing off the cedar walls of the judgment hall for more than an hour. If he whined the words *unfair taxes* one more time…

"So you see, your highness, these taxes are relatively unfair when considering—"

"Enough!" David's irritation boiled over.

The merchant stumbled backward. His scalded pride evidenced by the scarlet flushing of his round face.

Something squeezed in David's chest. The merchant wasn't the sole reason for his foul mood, and didn't deserve to bear the worst of it. "I'm sorry."

He wiped his forehead. Being the king of Israel was not what he'd hoped. He should be leading his army against the Philistines. Instead here he was, in his luxurious palace, listening to the endless and petty complaints. [1]

Ahithophel clapped his hands. "The king has heard enough of your whining for today. Come back later."

David stood and ran his hand through his hair. Loose curls

---

[1] 2 Sam 11:1

twisted around his fingers. He paced for a few moments before looking up. Amnon, his oldest son, glared over his shoulder as the aide shooed him out of the hall.

"Ahithophel, it's all right. I can…"

"My lord, their prattle is irritating me as well. It can wait until the morrow."

David ducked out the side exit, into the corridor to the private part of the palace. He stopped, inhaling the comforting scent of cedar, and waited for his aide.

Ahithophel slipped through the door and closed it quietly. His expression was tentative when he faced David.

"I am sorry, Ahithophel, but I am not cut of this pattern. I am the type of king who leads armies into battle, who destroys enemies, a king with a sword constantly by my side." He motioned to the warrior's blade hanging from his belt. "I love my people, but I cannot bear sitting here listening to their petty arguments while my army marches."

"My king, you know we can no longer risk you getting killed in some skirmish. Your sons are still young, and you have not yet determined a successor for your throne. If you were to fall in battle, Israel would be left in disarray."

David stepped closer to him and whispered through clenched teeth. "I can't do this. It's hard enough to stay here cooped up like a child, but listening to their trivial prattle day after day is more than I can stand."

Ahithophel gave him a sympathetic smile and laid a hand on his shoulder. "Take the remainder of the day to rest. Walk the gardens with your new wife, eat a good meal, refresh yourself.

You'll feel better tomorrow." He smiled again and disappeared down the hall.

Taking a deep breath, David wandered into the garden and wove through the trees and flowerbeds until he neared the fountain surrounded by pomegranate trees. The rich red fruit contrasted with the soft green of the olive leaves. The trickle of the water fountain and the sweet sound of turtledoves cooing soothed his soul. He should have brought his harp, for a psalm was bubbling up within him.

Standing in the midst of all this beauty was one not to be compared to it. With her emerald eyes set in a complexion of pearl, and ringlets of ruby cascading down her back. Bathsheba. He had loved her since the moment he saw her. His heart had sinned for her, bringing the wrath of his righteous God upon them. But although God had taken their baby, He had not denied him Bathsheba. [2]

Stepping beside her, David slid his hand into hers and gave it a tight squeeze.

"A rough day for my king?"

David groaned. "I am tired of being king. Can't I be something else for today?"

Bathsheba turned around. Her green eyes met his, and a smile curved her lips. She lifted his hands and placed them on her belly. "Then be Abba today."

The breath caught in his throat. "You're…"

---

[2] 2 Sam 11-12

By Amber Schamel

Her giggle and nod assured him it was so. Wrapping her in a tight embrace, he lifted her off her feet and whirled around in a circle. Finally setting her down, he placed his hands on either side of her face. "Blessed be the Lord God of Israel who has chosen in His great mercy to bless us. The child will be a son, and he will inherit my throne and reign over the house of Israel in peace and prosperity. There will be no one like him in all the world."

His wife's eyes sparkled in the light streaming through the trees. "Yes, our son will be a special child."

"When he is born, I will hold a feast a month long. The armies will rest from fighting to celebrate the birth of the prince of the house of David."

A frown contorted his wife's face. "But, if we announce at his birth that he will be your successor, won't it put him in danger?"

David's hands fell to his sides. He hadn't considered that. "You may be right. There must be another way." How could they appoint this child as the successor without endangering him? He could wait to announce it until later, but what if something happened to him in the meantime? No, wouldn't do. They had to come up with some sort of symbol. Something that wouldn't reveal the secret until the proper time. Something almost prophetic.

An idea ignited in his mind. Grasping Bathsheba's hand, he tugged her toward the palace. "Come. We have lots of work to do."

"David, what are you talking about?"

By Amber Schamel

"My son will not be wrapped in ordinary swaddling cloth. No, this prince is unlike any other child and must be treated as such. We will have cloth woven for him on the looms of Egypt, Sheba, Assyria, and every nation on the earth. At his birth, we will wrap him in swaddling clothes so magnificent no one will be able to deny his royalty. At my death, I shall decree that the son who possesses that certain cloth will be my heir. It will evade the danger, yet make it clear who I desire my heir to be. Quickly. We must find Ahithophel and have him gather merchants from every corner of the city."

*****

Maacah pressed her back against an olive trunk. Had she really heard right? All expected this new, young wife of David's would soon be with child, but how could the child of a commoner—a wife acquired through murder and iniquity—possibly be named the successor to the throne above her own son? Absalom was a beautiful child, beloved of all who knew him, third born, and of royal blood. What disgrace and insolence for David to consider this woman's son over Absalom. No, this could never be.

She peeked out from behind the tree as David led Bathsheba toward the palace. "Something must be done. That woman's son will never reign over Absalom."

Her thoughts raced like wild stallions as she darted toward her son's chambers. She didn't know how, but she would blight this plan to usurp Absalom's throne. Starting with the swaddling clothes.

*****

By Amber Schamel

David threw open the door to his aide's chamber. The energy he'd lost when his army marched from Jerusalem without him had returned. It felt good, and he was ready to commence his project.

His eyes swept the room. Across the bearskin rug stood a sturdy table. The man he sought hunched over it. "Ahithophel."

The aide looked up from the scrolls he studied. "Your highness, I didn't expect you back so soon."

"Where are my scribes?"

The man's eyebrow rose. "You dismissed them, sire."

"Yes. Well, I have a very important decree to issue. Summon the scribes at once."

"Begging your pardon, my lord, but isn't this a bit sudden?"

"Of course it's sudden. Isn't everything urgent sudden?" David could no longer hold back the grin spreading across his face. "Summon the scribes, my friend. Then I shall tell you the news."

Clapping his adviser on the back, he again took Bathsheba's hand and strode toward the court.

Ahithophel scrambled after them, barking the order over his shoulder. "Sire, please, what is this so urgent decree? What news? Is something wrong?"

David faced his friend as the guards opened the court's great doors. "No, my friend, not wrong, but something glorious. Come."

He settled on his throne, motioning Bathsheba to sit beside him. Ahithophel never could abide suspense, and his pained expression amused David.

By Amber Schamel

"My king, I could serve you better if you would enlighten me."

David opened his arms wide and lifted his gaze toward the heavens. "I am going to be an abba. Blessed be the name of the Lord!" His jubilant cry echoed through the corridor.

A puzzled frown crossed Ahithophel's face. Then his eyes drifted to Bathsheba. "Ah, mozel tov. Long life and happiness to the prince and his mother."

Shuffling in the doorway interrupted their conversation. Five scribes tiptoed into the hall, holding their writing instruments close to their chests.

David clapped twice. "It's about time. Take down a decree from the king."

Parchment rustled, and ink sloshed as the scribes scrambled to ready their tools. David extended a stocky finger toward the city as he issued his command. The scribes copied out his words and presented the documents. After David implanted his seal into the wax of each copy, the messenger carried them out of the hall. Horsemen would be waiting to carry the edict to each province of the land. Word would spread quickly, and he wouldn't have to wait long for tradesmen to begin flowing into the city.

*****

Absalom's resolute step carried him swiftly toward the court. His long tresses, curly like his father's, bounced against his broad shoulders. Could what Mother said be the truth? He refused to believe his father would plan to make Bathsheba's child his heir. For twenty years he had worked to become his

191

By Amber Schamel

father's favorite. She must have heard wrong. She did say she was a distance away as they spoke. He rounded the corner and entered the hall adjoining the throne room. A group of scribes stood in his way.

"You go in first. You're the one who has served the king the longest."

"He threw us out moments ago. Now he wants us back?"

Absalom rolled his eyes and brushed past them.

"I am going to be an abba! Blessed be the name of the Lord."

Absalom froze. The words unmistakably shouted in the king's voice. His *father's* voice.

He barely noticed the scribes bumping into him as they scurried through the doorway into the throne room. What could he mean by that? Was he not an abba already? Even with six sons?

Regaining his senses, Absalom peered around the door left ajar in the rush. King David's chest swelled. His finger extended toward where Absalom stood obscured by the door.

"Let it be written and posted throughout every city in the land of Israel: every craftsman skillful in the art of weaving is summoned to the palace in Jerusalem. The king and queen desire to fashion swaddling clothes for the prince of the house of David. The cloths will be of the finest thread, created from the best of every land. The craftsman selected will be paid a royal wage. A decree from David, king of Israel."

Swaddling clothes of the finest? Crafted from every land? Bile rose in Absalom's throat. His mother had been right. His own father was conspiring against his reign, in complete

By Amber Schamel

disregard of his heritage. He could not allow this. Something must be done. Something—but what?

Ready to continue the adventure?
Follow The Swaddling Clothes through time
and discover how they make their way into the
stable in Bethlehem.

Available now on Amazon or at
www.AmberSchamel.com.

By Amber Schamel

www.ingramcontent.com/pod-product-compliance
Lightning Source LLC
Chambersburg PA
CBHW020613120726
47905CB00003B/772